ℒℒ

PERSY
AND
THE PRINCE

PERSY
AND
THE PRINCE

•

Jane Myers Perrine

AVALON BOOKS
NEW YORK

PRINTED IN THE UNITED STATES OF AMERICA
ON ACID-FREE PAPER
BY HADDON CRAFTSMEN, BLOOMSBURG, PENNSYLVANIA

This book is dedicated to Ollie Perrine, my wonderful mother-in-law. Getting you in the bargain is one of the reasons I'm glad I married George.

And, of course, to George.

Chapter One

Persy Marsh was in trouble.

Feet stopped in front of where she knelt. They were large feet, shod in Gucci loafers, at least size eleven, she guessed. To her left, she was aware that the cocker spaniel's tail had begun to wag and knew what would happen as soon as the expensive shoes stopped in front of Cricket, an extremely friendly and excitable little dog.

Quickly Persy grabbed a magazine from the gold glass-topped table and slid it under Cricket's predictable bottom. As Persy had foreseen, Cricket's joy at seeing a new friend caused her to forget she was in the sumptuous lobby of the Gulf Prince Hotel. Persy cringed, certain the rug beneath Cricket's bottom cost more per square foot than Persy could earn in a month of dog walking. When the shoes turned toward the little dog, the inevitable happened.

Persy gave a sigh of relief as she realized she'd trapped every drop of the accident on the cover of the glitzy fashion magazine. Then she looked up at over six feet of dark elegance; the first time she'd ever thought to use that word to describe a man. As she looked into his icy gray eyes, she realized she held a soggy magazine with a damp puddle covering the smiling face of a high-priced model. Wasn't that the way it always was?

Even if she hadn't recognized him, the nameplate on the broad male chest—L. Jordan Prince, Manager— proclaimed his exalted rank. Persy grinned into his handsome but completely unamused face. It wore an expression of almost Victorian disapproval.

"Are you aware," he said in a cold voice with a slightly Eastern accent, "that the lobby is off-limits to dogs?"

"Yes, I am, and I do apologize," Persy began. "I'm Persy Marsh, the dog walker—"

"Are you not supposed to use the rear elevator and exit?" He used an even icier tone when he realized she wasn't a guest.

"Yes, and I do, always, except this one time. But this morning Cricket's leash broke." She tried to show him but holding the cocker by the collar with one hand and the oozing magazine in the other enabled her only to nod her head in the direction of the broken chain. "Before I could grab her, Cricket dashed in here. I'm afraid I had to chase her for a few minutes before I could catch her. I'll pay for any damage such as," she nodded again, "this magazine. If you'll give me a hand, I'll get her out of here."

"Very well. What can I do?"

She stood with Cricket under one arm and handed him the dripping magazine. "If you would just dispose of this," she said with what she hoped was an apologetic smile, "we'll leave."

She was almost to the rear exit when the arctic voice reached her ears. "I'd like to see you in my office when you return from the walk. Without the dog, of course."

"Yes, sir!" she shouted back. "Be careful! That glossy paper doesn't absorb much liquid." As the door closed behind her she relished a final glimpse of Jordan Prince glaring at the drops sliding off the magazine cover and onto the expensive floor.

"Imagine meeting Jordan Prince under such circumstances!" she said to the struggling dog. "And, you, you're such a problem," she lectured as she forced the links of the chain together by pressing the cheap metal against the wall. Completely unrepentant, Cricket wagged her tail and stared up at Persy, her head to one side. "But you do help pay the bills so we might as well get your walk finished."

When Jordan Prince first spotted the slight figure, all he could see was a riot of gold curls. He thought the person was a young boy with execrably cut hair and sniffed patronizingly at the sight of such a ragamuffin in the lobby of the Gulf Prince. But when he spotted the dog, he stalked toward the pair, becoming more furious with each step that this urchin would have a creature in the lobby of his hotel. Opening his mouth to blast this being, he looked down into a pair of cornflower blue eyes peering out of a face of unusual loveliness, surrounded by ridiculously uncontrolled curls. Then she'd stood. She was tiny, and certainly wasn't a young boy, thought the connoisseur of feminine charm. She was slender but nicely rounded.

He enjoyed watching her for a moment before reminding himself that this delicious little armful, no matter how lovely, was not for him. He was a man around whom women flocked, drawn by his family name, physical attributes, and more than comfortable fortune.

He saw her glance at him and had stood there, supremely confident of his ability to intimidate this young woman, only to have the disgustingly saturated magazine thrust into his hand. Furious at her lack of respect and the drips that marred the shining elegance of his shoes, he bellowed for the bellman and shoved the slimy periodical at him.

Jordan made Persy wait five minutes after his receptionist announced her. He expected her to be ill at ease, but she entered his office with a grace both seductive and innocent. She looked like a child in the enormous chair, sublimely indifferent to the picture she made. He wasn't. He couldn't keep his eyes away from her.

"Yes?" Persy asked with a confidence he hadn't expected.

"I see," he said as he turned the pages of her employment file, "that you've been employed by the hotel off and on for three years: dealer in the casino, lifeguard, waitress."

"Anything that comes up, sir."

Jordan lifted an eyebrow and looked at her. He couldn't believe the "sir" was a genuine sign of respect but her face betrayed nothing. "Why haven't I seen you before?"

"I work odd shifts and I always try to stay in my place, sir."

"To stay in your place?" He lifted an eyebrow in question.

"You know—an underling, a servant, a flunky. My mother did try to teach me proper behavior, but I fear, sir, there are times I am woefully lacking in manners."

He ignored the comments and leafed through the pages of her file. He found there only a list of jobs she'd filled, her age, and the fact that she was single and lived in El Valle, the slightly seedy area near the hotel where many of the employees lived.

"Miss Marsh?"

"Yes, sir."

"Could you please explain your presence in the lobby?"

"Which part," she asked with great respect, "of what I explained earlier didn't you understand?"

"How did you get in the lobby?"

"Cricket ran in there after her chain broke."

"How did the dog get through the double doors?"

"Oh, the double doors. Those doors that keep the riffraff on one side, away from the guests? Well, some careless person must have left them open because we riffraff just walked right in."

"You realize that you weren't supposed to be there?"

"I did, sir, but Cricket seemed a little confused. Of course, she's a cocker of very little brain. I've found all of that breed to be foolish but loveable creatures."

Certainly she couldn't be laughing at him. He

caught a trembling of her lips and a sparkle in her eyes before she brought her features under control. He had nothing more to say to her. In fact, he'd never had anything to say to her. Why had he insisted that she come to his office when she made him feel like an idiot?

Well, he'd wanted to see her again. That wasn't hard to understand. She was pretty, but the main reason he was attracted was that she seemed so different from the women he usually met. Besides, he thought with a carefully hidden grin, he enjoyed her attitude a little even though he had no idea how to react to it.

"Do you want me to pay for the magazine?" She opened her change purse. "I don't believe there was any other damage."

"No, no, that won't be necessary." They sat in silence for a minute. She looked at him expectantly while he pretended to study her file.

"Is there anything else?" she prompted.

And he couldn't think of anything else.

"No, that's all." He stood and moved around his desk to walk her to the door. Opening it, he said as she left, "And don't let the dogs into the lobby again," for the benefit of the receptionist.

"Aye, aye, sir," she answered.

Persy looked at her watch. Goodness, it was almost three o'clock. She still had to check on a job, go to the grocery store, and get home to fix dinner for Agatha Norton. After that, maybe she could relax for an hour or two.

When she'd completed the errands and opened the door of the small but well-kept house, it was five o'clock. She could hear Willie Nelson's latest complaint coming from Agatha's bedroom.

"Agatha, I'm home." Persy knocked on the door of the front bedroom. "Dinner will be ready in a few minutes."

Agatha had owned the house before Persy rented it. A nephew, the executor of Agatha's deceased husband's estate, had made arrangements for Agatha in a nice nursing home. Unfortunately, the nursing home refused to take Barbarella, Agatha's skinny, fussy cat, and Agatha refused to go without her so the nephew paid Persy to watch out for the elderly woman. Agatha lived in the front bedroom while Persy stayed in the back bedroom—the very small back bedroom.

"I was afraid you weren't going to be home in time." Agatha strode into the kitchen. "You know I don't like to get to bingo late."

"I know. Dinner's almost ready." Persy stirred the soup. "If you'll set the table, we can eat a little earlier." She looked over at Agatha, who wore a new pink dress with ruffles around the neck.

"Don't you look pretty." Persy studied the older woman for a minute. "Agatha, why are you so devoted to bingo lately? Now you go every time the hall is open, always all dressed up. Do you have a boyfriend there?"

"Hrmph." She took the silverware from a drawer and dropped it on the table.

"I think that's wonderful. Why don't you tell me about him?"

"Didn't say I did. Didn't say I didn't." Agatha muttered. "Didn't say anything."

Knowing nothing would get Agatha to talk if she didn't want to, Persy asked, "Has Susan been by?"

"Yes, she left you some information on the literacy campaign and the new candidate for city council. Lot of nonsense." Agatha put napkins next to the spoons. "And she wonders if you can sit her kids tonight."

"Of course. What else do I have to do?"

"Well, Frank came by. Says he needs help in trig tonight."

"Wonderful! I was afraid I was going to have an evening to myself for once!" Persy poured soup into bowls and carried them to where Agatha sat.

"You're always doing something to help. Don't know why. Guess you have to keep yourself busy. Guess you'd be bored if you had an evening to yourself."

"I don't know. I can't remember the last time I had one!"

Chapter Two

"You promise me these nails won't fall off?" Persy sat at the kitchen table in Susan Moreno's house a few days later. She peeled the back off a fake fingernail and pushed it onto her thumbnail.

"I didn't promise that," Susan said. "Mine don't fall off but I'm careful. I don't do the crazy things you do."

She kept pressure on the thumbnail as she looked around the small kitchen and living room. "Where's your husband?"

"He heard you were coming over and left."

"I wish we got along better." Persy studied her index finger.

"Yeah, both of you do. You wish he'd stop being so bossy and he wishes you would."

"I really like them." Persy looked at the long orange nails with tiny cats in the corners. "Of course, they're really Halloween nails and that's why they were so cheap but I think they look good with our new uniforms." Persy motioned toward the black uniform she wore to serve at catered parties. "There!" Persy finished pressing on the last nail and held her hands out. "What do you think?"

"Interesting. Will you be able to pick up plates and glasses with them?"

"Let me see." Persy cleared the table and placed the dishes in the sink. "It just takes holding the dishes a little differently, sort of sideways, but I can do it." She glanced at the clock. "Hey, I'd better get going. It's late." She ran out of Susan's house and started toward the hotel.

"Okay, Pers, you and Maria will serve while Kim sets up the kitchen. This is important. Mr. Prince will be there. It's the quarterly meeting of the Board of Directors of the hotel chain," Hogan, the special events caterer, explained.

With special care, Persy took plates of salad from the dumbwaiter, put them on the tables, and filled glasses with tea. "I think everything looks great."

"We're ready for them," Maria said.

When Jordan ushered the board members into the room, Persy saw his eyes slide across her with only a quick smile to show recognition. When the diners were seated, the waitresses served bowls of the chef's renowned black bean and snapper soup.

Oh, darn, Persy thought as she looked at the bowl of soup she'd just placed before Jordan. Her orange nail floated on the top. She tried to reach over him and remove the dish, but Jordan looked up and said, "Don't take my soup, Miss Marsh. I haven't started it yet." His eyes fell to the orange nails still attached to her fingers. He blinked when he saw them before turning to speak with the woman on his right.

When he picked up his spoon and started to dip into the soup, Persy held her breath. He was going to see it soon. Would he fire her on the spot? Would he yell at her?

But he didn't see it. He wasn't even looking at the soup as he talked with the board members. Little by little, the orange object began to sink.

Maybe it would sink to the bottom and he wouldn't notice, Persy hoped. No, he'd probably dip it up with his spoon and swallow it without even noticing. It'd get caught in his throat. She'd have to do the Heimlich maneuver and, when the nail popped out of his mouth, he'd know who'd almost killed him.

Or maybe he'd swallow it and it would get caught some place inside, doing some terrible internal damage. When they did surgery or—could it come to this?—an autopsy, they'd find her nail. Perhaps by that time she could dispose of the rest but someone was likely to remember.

Even though she didn't like him much, she didn't want to cause him pain. She certainly didn't want to kill him.

Finally, the suspense ended when he saw the orange fragment on top of a bean. "What is . . . ?" He looked up as Persy trotted around the table to take his bowl. "Yes, Miss Marsh, I believe you'd better take this." He looked at her nails again as he passed her the soup. His lips twitched but he refused to meet her eyes.

"Was he angry?" Maria asked when Persy had time to tell her what had happened at the end of the meal.

"I don't know. He didn't say anything. I was going

to apologize but he actually gave me a little smile when he left. I don't think I'm going to wear these." She waved toward the nails she'd pulled off and thrown in the trash. "Never again."

"He smiled?"

"Yeah, maybe he's not as uptight as I used to think."

"Miss Marsh, may I talk to you in the hall?"

Persy jumped when she heard his voice behind her. Certainly he hadn't heard what she'd said, had he?

"Yes, sir." She followed him out of the kitchen.

Jordan watched Persy for a moment. She seemed nervous, probably thought he was going to get on her about the nails and how dangerous they could be, but that wasn't why he'd asked her to come with him. In fact, he didn't have the slightest idea what he was going to say or why he'd asked her into the hall—except that he really wanted to see her again.

Finally he surprised himself by asking, "Would you go to dinner with me this evening?"

She straightened and turned slowly toward him, her eyes opened wide. "What?"

"I asked you to go to dinner with me this evening."

"Why?"

"Heaven only knows!" he blurted.

"How flattering."

She was laughing again, he thought, and he dared not tell her why he wanted to see her, that he was terribly attracted to her. She'd really laugh at that. "I'd like to have dinner with you, Miss Marsh."

"I can't imagine why. After all, you're the manager of the hotel. I'm only a dog walker."

"I doubt you've reached the age of . . ." he tried to remember what her file had said, "twenty-five without a great number of men wanting to take you to dinner. I'd imagine my reasons are little different from theirs."

"I imagine you're right!" Persy had an enormous grin. "I know exactly why most men want to take me out. Are you saying your reasons are purely physical? I mean, we've hardly had time to develop any other type of relationship."

"Well, no, not exactly. I mean—"

"I doubt we'd have much to talk about. After all, you're the manager. Your family owns lots and lots of Prince Hotels whereas I enter and leave by the rear entrance," she said humbly, head down. "On the other side of the double doors." She looked up and he could see her wide and completely delightful smile.

"Yes, I do find you attractive. Would you have dinner with me tonight?"

"I'd like to have dinner with you but I can't tonight. It's bingo night."

"Do you play bingo? I thought that was for the elderly."

"Agatha does. Is tomorrow night all right?"

"Fine. I'll pick you up at seven."

"I live at 106 La Paloma, in El Valle. Please don't plan anything too fancy. I don't have the clothes to go to the roof garden."

Jordan couldn't remember being on a street like this before—oh, he'd driven past them, but never walked down their narrow and broken sidewalks. On the north side of La Paloma, tidy houses faced the parking lots on the back of the hotel. They were neat enough, well cared for. Most were painted white, each with a tiny flower patch in front. Number 106 was no larger or smaller than the others. It was white, too, and square. In front was a tiny porch with a swing. He knocked and waited.

"Hello, Mr. Prince." An elderly woman opened the door. "Persy's coming."

Jordan entered the house and gave a slight nod in the woman's direction. "Delighted to meet you. Are you Miss Marsh's grandmother?"

"Nothing like that." The woman glanced up from the sandwiches she was fixing.

"I sort of inherited Agatha." Persy came from the back of the house wearing a sort of floaty dress and looking terrific in a floating sort of way.

Before he could speak, a scrawny gray cat ambled up to Jordan and twisted herself around his ankles, leaving fur on his socks.

"Who is this?" Jordan asked between clenched teeth while surreptitiously attempting to push the creature away from him.

"That's Barbarella, Agatha's cat. You might as well forget about getting rid of her. Obviously, you don't like cats."

"Well, no—"

"I mean, it *is* obvious. Barbarella senses who doesn't like cats and gets very loving around them." She watched Jordan's discomfort before she picked the cat up and put her on the sofa. "Shall we go?" Persy tilted her head and glanced up at him with her enormously blue eyes.

Not even a hint of make-up on them, no liner, no

mascara, nothing to make them look larger. She didn't need that.

"Where're you going for dinner?" Agatha said as she cut her sandwich. "Bring me back a doggie bag."

"If I can." Persy patted the elderly woman's shoulder.

Jordan reached around her to open the door, and they were soon at the end of the short driveway. "I hope you don't mind if we walk. The restaurant is just down the street from the hotel." He followed her as she turned instinctively toward their place of employment.

"No, I love to walk."

Silence, complete silence fell and Jordan didn't know how to break it. Why had he asked her to dinner? They had nothing in common, nothing to talk about, and he couldn't help but wish they did.

He hadn't known where to take her. The hotel was out—he didn't think taking her to Prince's Prime, their finest bistro, was wise. It would impress her but, after all, she was a hotel employee and the gossip would be unfortunate. Even the coffee shop was out. And the country club—well, she had warned him that she didn't have the clothes to go someplace fancy.

"Oh, wait a minute."

Surprised to hear her finally say something, Jordan turned to see Persy fumbling in her purse in front of a man selling flowers. "I would have brought flowers if I'd known you wanted them," he said.

"I didn't want to have to tell you I'd like flowers." She chose a yellow and blue bunch that matched her dress and gently rubbed her hand over the petals. They walked in silence until he stopped in front of the Burning Embers.

"I've heard this is good," she said when he opened the door for her. Jordan scrutinized the dining room with a practical eye. Chairs upholstered in burgundy sat around heavy wooden tables with candles. On the walls were prints of flowers while soft music established a soothing atmosphere. He nodded. This was fine. Not too fancy but pleasant.

After a hostess led them to their table and handed them menus, Jordan seated Persy and sat across from her.

"Do you come here often?" Persy asked, breaking the silence.

Jordan glanced up from his menu and studied Persy. She'd put her menu on the table and was weaving the flowers together in a little crown. When she finished, she smiled at him and placed the wreath on her head. It looked amazingly fetching on her unruly curls. He'd never seen anything like the long, loose dress she wore. There was lace around the neck and the material was covered in flowers, tiny blue flowers that matched her eyes, eyes that made him forget her question.

"What did you say?"

"I said, do you come here often?"

"No. My secretary recommended it. She said the food's good."

She nodded before she studied her menu again. "I'm not sure what to order." She glanced up. "I'm guessing price is no object."

"Well, of course not." She smiled at him and he realized she was teasing him again. Because he still didn't know how to react, he smiled back. That seemed to satisfy her.

After they ordered and were served their salads, Jordan said, "So, how did your day go?" He couldn't believe he'd said that. He prided himself on carrying on intelligent conversation but now he sounded like his mother had when grilling him.

"Fine." She nodded.

"What did you do?"

"Oh, made a few beds, vacuumed a few floors, swam some laps, and looked for another job."

"Another job? Why do you need another job? You're always working."

"I need the money."

"Couldn't you find one job that paid enough?"

"I'm easily bored. I like variety and freedom." She finished her salad, pushed it away, then looked up at him, her hands folded under her chin and her eyes fixed firmly on his face. "What did you do today?"

His mouth suddenly became dry. Lost in her blue gaze, he couldn't think of anything to say, not one word. After a few seconds, he said, "Oh, not much. I called some people."

"Made a few deals?"

He nodded.

With the conversation flowing a bit, they chatted a little between bites. About the weather. The hotel. The guests. Their hotel. But, at least they weren't sitting in silence anymore. As he thought that, Jordan heard a soft voice.

"Hey, mister." Startled, Jordan looked down at the little person who stood next to his chair. He put a grubby hand on Jordan's jacket and continued to speak. "Hi, mister."

"I beg your pardon?"

"Hello." The child continued to stare up at Jordan with an angelic expression before he tried to climb onto his immaculate white trousers.

Jordan was momentarily stunned. Never had anyone made such an assault on him. "I'm not really a person who likes children," he explained as he attempted to move the child off his trousers after he had left a dirty footprint and sticky smudges. As he did this, a woman hurried up to the table and removed the child.

"Andrew, how many times have I told you—" A chubby brunette held the squirming child. "I apologize, sir. He's too friendly and I have to keep an eye on him. I think he really likes you."

Terrific.

The brunette turned toward Persy and a brilliant smile lit her face. "Persy! How wonderful to see you. What are you doing here?"

"Hi, Barb. Great to see you. It has to be six months already. Hasn't Andrew grown?" Persy motioned to Jordan, who stood stiffly. "Jordan, this is my friend Barb Perez. Barb, I want you to meet Jordan Prince. He's treating me to dinner."

He held out his hand before he realized Barb's were both full with her son.

"Nice to meet you." Barbara nodded at him before turning back to Persy. "Listen, I finished that great training program you found for me. You won't believe this, but I've had two job offers and am deciding between them now. Can you imagine? I have a choice now!"

"Great, Barb. I'm really happy for you."

"My husband brought us here to celebrate." Barb glanced at Jordan then back at Persy again. "I'd better go and leave you to your date, but I wanted to tell you."

"Call me." After her friend left, Persy finished the last bite of steak and sat back. "Thank you. That was really nice."

"Would you like dessert?" He handed her the card on the table.

"No, but I would like a cup of coffee. Maybe an espresso?"

They spent almost twenty minutes sipping coffee and carrying on halting conversation before he said, "If you're finished, I'll pay the check." He motioned toward the waiter and handed him a credit card.

"Where to now?" Persy asked as they left the restaurant and looked at the descending sun. "Dancing at your country club? Painting the town, hopping from one chic cabaret to another in your Rolls?"

"Well, no. I really had no other plans."

"Ah, you were thinking, perhaps, of your suite at the hotel?"

"Of course not! I hadn't thought of any place. I've been busy lately." And he'd really had no idea what they should do after dinner but babbling hadn't been part of the plan.

"Mr. Prince, how popular you must be. What excitement you put in the lives of the women you date! First, dinner, followed by spontaneous fun." She looked at him out of the corner of her eye before saying in a less sarcastic tone, "Why don't we walk on the beach? It really is one of my favorite ways to spend time—when I have it."

"I'm not sure." Jordan looked at his glossy shoes.

"Come on." She took his hand and led him toward the ocean. "You act as if you've never walked the beach."

"When I was a child . . . and, of course, I have been swimming at beaches."

"You have this beautiful beach." She flung her arms out and waved toward the area. "Right outside the hotel and you've never watched the sun go down or the moon reflected in the water or gotten up early to glory in the sunrise?"

"I'm afraid I don't glory all that much."

His words brought a delightful laugh from her.

"Of course," he continued, "you can't miss the moon but I usually see that from the front veranda."

She was holding his hand and doing some sort of little dance of joy. Her smile left sparkles in the air that seemed to explode before his eyes. How did she do that?

By the time the two arrived at the beach, the sun had almost set and the sky was getting darker. "Isn't it fantastic? Look at the colors in the ocean. Isn't it the most wonderful, glorious sight you've ever seen?" She kicked off her sandals and made a dash across the sand, closing her eyes, holding out her arms, and squeezing the sand between her toes. Then she returned to him and, grasping his hand, she pulled him onto the sand and swung him around and around.

"Persy, my shoes."

"Don't wear shoes to walk on the beach. You have

to feel the warmth beneath your feet, the sand between your toes. Sit!"

When he had seated himself and pulled off his shoes and socks, she took them from him and placed them under the boardwalk.

"You're going to love this." She pranced away from him. "Now you can run along the water's edge with me."

He tried again to grab her but before he could capture her, Persy danced out of his reach.

"You're going to have to catch me," she taunted. "If you want me, you're going to have to chase me." She dashed off across the sand.

Chapter Three

Jordan tried to close the distance between himself and the willowy shape that moved farther and faster away. In the dusk, he saw Persy trip over the hem of her dress as she pranced through the waves lapping the beach. He gained on her and grasped her hand as she tried to regain her footing. Her feet tangled in the dress, she lost her balance. He fell next to her on the wet sand bordering the warm water. Before Jordan could pull her against him, she leaped to her feet.

But he was faster. He pulled her back down next to him and dropped his mouth on hers. Her lips were soft and sweet. Then a wave broke against them and left him sputtering.

She looked up at him. In the disappearing light, he could see her eyes were wide. He kissed her again. She tasted like coffee and saltwater.

She sat up and pushed him away. "No."

"What do you mean, 'no?' "

"I'm sorry. I need to get home." She started away from him. "This is moving too fast."

"Persy?"

She turned, but he didn't know what he'd meant to say.

"I want to see you again." The words popped out of his mouth.

"Why?" When he didn't answer, she continued, "Don't pretend you like me. I know you don't! You don't take a woman you like to dinner and have nothing planned for the rest of the evening. You don't tell a woman you like that you don't know why you asked her out!"

"I'm sorry about that. I was rude."

Persy went on as if he'd never spoken. "I don't know why I'd ever want to go out with you again. You affect me somehow. I can't explain it. I look at you and see everything I dislike in a man—"

Jordan broke in. "Are you going to leave me any pride at all? After all, I did ask you out again."

"Yes, but I don't think you really wanted to. My problem is that I'm attracted to you, and I can't figure out why."

When she shook her head, a gust of wind picked up the wreath of flowers and gently moved it, draping it over her forehead.

He watched as her eyelashes tangled in the woven flowers before he lifted it carefully and dropped it back on her curls. For a moment he stared into her eyes before she turned away again.

"Tonight I behaved badly, teasing you and running

away from you, all over the beach." She looked at him over her shoulder. "I'm sorry."

"Oh, darn. What am I supposed to do now?"

"You could forgive me." She turned around to study him then moved away from him, hopping backwards.

"I don't know. I probably should but I don't know how to react to you. I don't know what you're going to do or say and that can be very uncomfortable." He strode down the beach and stood in front of her for a moment before saying. "And very exciting. You confuse me greatly."

Behind her, streetlights from the hotel glowed around her like an aura, shimmering off her brilliant curls.

"We seem to have an odd effect on each other," Persy agreed.

"You're probably as confused by this relationship—can we even call this a relationship?—as I am."

"We probably should never see each other again." She walked past him, toward El Valle.

"Probably not, ever."

She looked up at him with those incredibly blue eyes, her lips glistening in the moonlight. He leaned over and brushed her lips with his. "Go on, you'd better get back home. It's late and I have to find my shoes and socks."

She glanced toward La Paloma, then back at him.

"You'll be fine alone. I can see your house from here. I'll watch to make sure you get home safely. Besides," he motioned toward his wet and sandy trousers, "I'm in no shape to be seen by anyone."

Jordan watched Persy dance across the moon shadows on the sand, her figure gracefully moving like a whitecapped wave against the shore. She stopped to pick up her shoes, waved toward him, and then twirled out of his sight.

"Darn," he muttered, looking at himself. His white slacks and pink shirt were wet, covered with sand. Keeping an eye on Persy, he stumbled over to the boardwalk to get his shoes. As she disappeared into her neighborhood, he found them.

Feeling more ridiculous than he could ever remember, he returned to the hotel and snuck in the back entrance, leaving a trail of sand behind him.

The next morning, Agatha packed a lunch for Persy and whistled. Suspicious of Agatha's unusually good mood, Persy asked, "Agatha, do you have a boyfriend at bingo?" At Agatha's refusal to answer, Persy continued, "It's true! There *is* a gentleman. Who is he? Will he call on you?"

"No," Agatha snorted. "He comes on a van from the retirement community up the coast. They come to play bingo. We've gotten to be good friends. His name is Burt. Not nearly as handsome as that Jordan fellow but not so uptight either."

"That's a pretty good description of Jordan."

"Oh, I know why you see him. Looking at you it was like watching a magnet trying to stay away from a piece of metal. I bet he was all over you when you got away from here."

"Agatha!"

"Well, wasn't he? Even an old lady can pick up on that strong an attraction. Where'd he take you for dinner? Someplace fancy?"

"The Burning Embers."

"Nice enough but he could afford better." Agatha put the knife down. "Only wanted your body, huh?"

"Agatha!"

"Drop him. There're a lot nicer fellows around."

Agatha was right. There were lots of nice guys around. There was Keith at the law office who seemed interested. Stan at the reception desk had asked her out for coffee. So had several of the lifeguards, but they were too young.

Why wasn't she interested in any of them? And why was she so attracted to Jordan? She could kid herself and say that beneath his patronizing attitude there was a nicer, better person, but she had no proof of that. None at all.

So, why? Was the feeling left over from her past? Was the choice of a rich snob hereditary? He was good-looking, sure, but so were Stan and Keith. The lifeguards were absolutely gorgeous. If she were smart, she'd take Agatha's advice.

Instead, she took the brown bag Agatha handed her and headed toward the hotel, wondering if she would see him.

"Good morning," Persy bobbed her head at the departing guests as she pushed the cleaning cart down the hall. The tiny, stiff maid's hat wobbled on her curls.

The wheels of the cart shrieked when she pushed it. As hard as she pushed, it headed toward the center of the hall instead of the side. With a shove, she forced its mass out of the way of anyone in the corridor.

She took out her keys, knocked and, when no one answered, opened the door to room 312. With towels and linens in hand, she entered the room. Tossing them on the dresser, Persy quickly stripped the beds and began to make them. She shook out the bottom sheet and, working with speed and efficiency, quickly tucked it in. She'd just thrown the top sheet and blanket on the bed when a voice came from the door.

"Have you been trained in how to make the Prince Hotel's tight corner, Miss Marsh?"

Persy turned to see Russell O'Neal, the head housekeeper. Behind him, Jordan leaned against the wall, looking tall, handsome, and totally in charge. Persy fingered the curls that escaped from her cap but realized there was nothing she could do about her disheveled appearance. Why did he have to look so good?

"Yes, sir, I have," Persy said to the housekeeper.

"May I see you do it?"

Persy tucked the top sheet in according to Prince Hotel regulations. "There, sir."

O'Neal strode to the bed, tapped the tautness of the bedclothes and noted the sharp crease of the corners. "That's how all beds are to be done, Miss Marsh."

"Yes, sir, except this one."

"Without exception, Miss Marsh. Had I not happened to walk by and seen you tossing that blanket on top of a sheet without square corners, our guests would have had," he paused for effect, "sloppy bedding."

"I shudder to contemplate that, sir, and assure you I do make the Prince Hotel's tight corners in every other room. However, this one is an exception."

"Miss Marsh, this is how beds are made at the Gulf Prince Hotel." He pointed at the tight corners.

"Even if the guests request otherwise, sir?"

"I beg your pardon?"

"Yesterday, the guests in this room told me they don't like tight corners, sir, because they both have arthritis, sir. If the sheets are too tight across their feet, it's painful for them to pull the corners out themselves. They asked that I not tuck in the corners, sir." By this time, Persy was beginning to feel like a cadet at West Point.

"Oh, well, in that case." Jordan entered the room. "Congratulations on serving our guests so well." He turned toward the housekeeper to say, "You may go, Russell. I will discuss this with Miss Marsh."

"Yes, sir." O'Neal turned to leave.

"What are you doing here? I didn't realize you were a maid also." Jordan turned to Persy.

"I'm filling in." She went into the bathroom to hang the towels and to straighten and wipe the counter before she brought clean glasses in from the cart. Jordan watched.

"Am I keeping you from your job?"

"Oh, no, sir. Go ahead and talk while I'm cleaning. I have to be down at the pool as soon as I finish here." She glanced at him as she dusted the surfaces.

"Why are you here?" Persy asked as she went into the hall, wrestled the vacuum in, and plugged it into the outlet.

"O'Neal wanted me to survey the maids with him today; however, I think he's a little embarrassed at his wasted officiousness. I thought I'd allow him time to pull himself together before we continued the walk through." He moved toward the door. "And thank you."

"For what?" Persy turned off the vacuum so she could hear him.

"For caring about the guests. For listening to them."
He smiled, a sincere smile that stunned her.

"And that's important to you?"

"Very important, Miss Marsh," he said as he left the room.

He'd been nice. Jordan Prince had been nice to her.

"Miss Marsh, your cart is too far out in the hall."

Darn it, that cart was only two inches from the wall. But, he was her boss. "I'll move it, sir." She glared at him as he walked toward the elevators.

After he entered one, he turned toward her and smiled. She glowered as he disappeared behind the closing door.

"Darn you, Jordan Prince," she mumbled. Just when she'd started thinking better about the man, he ruined it by being himself.

"What did you say?"

She turned to see Susan standing only a foot behind her. "Oh, nothing."

"What's going on between you and the Prince? I heard you guys went out to dinner the other night."

Persy went back into the room and started to vacuum. After a few seconds of shouting, Susan unplugged the machine.

"Is there anything I should know?"

Franny frowned at her, too. Probably not a good idea. It would leave wrinkles on her forehead and she'd look old before she really was. All because of Jordan Prince.

"I said," Susan interrupted her thoughts, "what's going on with you and the Prince? You'd better tell me."

"Or?"

"Or I won't help you with your last rooms and you'll be late to the pool."

"Oh, that's a good friend. Besides, there's nothing going on so I have nothing to tell you," Persy lied as she tried to reach past Susan to plug the vacuum in again.

Susan didn't move.

"Oh, all right." Persy stood. "There really isn't anything going on. He took me to dinner but it was really uncomfortable. He hasn't asked me out again, although he sort of started to but he didn't finish. Besides, he's officious and pretentious and a stuffed shirt. Everything I hate in a man."

"Yeah, but he sure is pretty."

"Pretty is as pretty does."

"Lordy, Persy, I never thought you'd say such a stupid thing."

"I didn't either but the man—" She shrugged. "I don't know. He really is everything I don't like in a man, but . . ."

"It's like calling like."

Persy's glance flew to Susan's face. "What do you mean?"

"Like calling like. You're both from hotsy-totsy society families, as much as you try to pretend you aren't. You're both incredibly over-educated. Like I said, like calling like."

"I'm not like him. Not a bit. I mean, I am educated, but I needed those degrees to do what I like to do. And I live on my own money, thank you. I get nothing from my family."

"And you love driving them crazy about that." Susan nodded. "Okay, girl, I'll start on your last room while you finish up here. And don't you ever say I'm not acting like your friend. That's what friends do."

"Lecture and stick your nose into my life?"

"Exactly." Susan jingled her keys as she left.

"Where're you working today?" Agatha asked as she made Persy's lunch a few days later.

"I'm lifeguarding this morning then dealing this afternoon." Persy picked up her uniform and took a brown bag. "I'll see you later!" She turned and ran up the street and through the narrow path between the banks of thick bushes that separated El Valle from the hotel property.

"Someone's going to get killed here one day." Susan passed her going the other way, just getting off the night shift. "I'm always glad when I go through here during the day."

"I know," Persy agreed.

"Somebody's going to get robbed 'cause that hotel's too cheap to put up lights and make this safe. Listen, Persy, when you have to come home late at night, you call me. I'll have one of the guys watch for you."

"Thanks, Susan. See you!"

There were a few early risers waiting to swim when Persy opened the gate. She covered her skin with sunscreen, rubbed zinc oxide on her nose, and climbed into the lifeguard perch to watch the guests swim and dive.

"Mr. Prince, are you aware that some of your employees have requested a meeting with the hotel administration about the conditions of the walkway between here and El Valle?" Harold Sanchez, head of the legal department, spread out some papers on Jordan's desk. "We have received about thirty letters from residents of El Valle requesting that the area be made safer."

"My understanding is—and correct me if I'm wrong, Harold—that this passage is not one that the hotel has set up but one that hotel employees have used on their own for a number of years."

"I believe you have asked the employees not to use this passage."

"That's true. Besides, the employees could go out the front of the hotel, down to the end of the block, turn, and go home that way. Many do. That way is lighted all the way by the city. Is that correct?"

"Yes, sir. However, those employees who leave through the front of the hotel live on the street next to the hotel so that exit is more convenient. Those who live behind the hotel would add a seven- to ten-minute walk, from what the letters say."

"Are we required to spend hotel funds to make this more convenient?"

"There are two answers to that question, sir: yes and no. However, it would be nice for the hotel to spend that money for a situation that concerns the employees' safety. It would probably be good for morale and cooperation."

"We pay better than any employer on the Gulf, Harold. I would think that would be excellent for morale. Go on."

"In one of the letters, written by a Persistence Marsh . . ." The lawyer paused to go through the stack before he pulled out a neatly typed missive.

Jordan jumped when he heard the name. Surely Persy Marsh and Persistence Marsh must be the same person. What had Persy written? It was hard to guess.

"May I see that?" Jordan asked in a calm voice.

Harold passed it to Jordan. "You'll notice that she brings up a very important legal point: right of way. Have the employees been using that passage for long enough that it is a legal right of way and cannot be closed? If so, should it be maintained by the hotel because it is hotel property? It's an interesting consideration."

Jordan perused the letter. "I wonder where she got her legal information."

"A very sound argument, sir. Well-stated and precise. Is this Ms. Marsh employed by the hotel?"

"Sporadically."

"May I suggest, sir, that none of these people—and I have a list of those who wrote letters—should continue in their employment if they continue to cause problems for the hotel."

"Are you suggesting that I tell the employees to shut up or lose their jobs?"

"Oh, no, sir. I'd never suggest that you tell the employees exactly that. It would leave us open to lawsuits. However, I believe you could practice that without actually making threats. It would be very effective in keeping down dissent."

Jordan stood and looked out the window. He could see Persy sitting in the lifeguard chair. "Harold, I believe in the right of the employee to state concerns. I may not agree with them, and do find complaints bothersome, but I uphold that right."

"Very well, sir. I'll keep you informed as this develops."

"Thanks, Harold."

After the lawyer left, Jordan again looked from the window of his office. "Martha," he said to his secretary. "Call the pool and ask Miss Marsh to come see me when she has a break."

"Yes, sir."

Jordan watched the top of Persy's curls. He wasn't sure exactly what he planned to say to her, but he was intrigued by her impressive letter. He went back to his desk and dictated a few more letters to Martha until there was a knock on the door.

"Mr. Prince? You wanted to see me?" Persy had pulled a T-shirt over her suit. Her feet were in scuffed sandals.

"Come in and sit down, Miss Marsh. You may leave, Martha. I don't want to be disturbed for awhile."

When the secretary left, Persy asked, "Yes, sir?"

"When I was talking to the lawyer for the Prince chain, he told me you wrote our legal department about a concern." He leaned toward her.

"Yes, sir. I'm worried about the area between the hotel and El Valle."

"He showed me your letter. I was most impressed. Where did you learn so much about the law?"

"I'm a neighborhood organizer in El Valle. We have lawyers who volunteer time and their legal knowledge."

"What does a neighborhood organizer do?"

"I try to make life better for the people who live there. Communicate, get them information they need, represent them at council and board meetings. Most of them can't take off for the meetings. That's why I work the odd hours I do."

"Very interesting." It was no use. Try as he might to listen to Persy, as he watched her soft lips move, he wanted to kiss them. He tried to pay attention to her speech but he found his eyes resting on her mouth again. Without a word, he stood and walked around the desk, took Persy's hand and drew her up from the chair and into his arms. Before he could kiss her, his world exploded in pain.

"No!" Persy shouted.

"You kicked me." Jordan reached for his throbbing shin in amazement. "That hurt."

"It hurt me, too!" Persy held onto the sore toes protruding over the edge of the sandal. "But I will not be kept on the premises for your pleasure any time you whistle for me! I'm not a tramp."

"I wasn't—" he began then stopped, knowing she was right.

"I could report this as sexual harassment."

"I'm not . . . I mean, I wouldn't."

"But I don't think it is. I think it's only amazing chemistry between two people who have absolutely nothing else in common and don't know what to do about it."

"Persy, I'm really sorry. I looked out and saw you at the pool, and I wanted to see you. I was an idiot but this has nothing to do with your job. You don't have to do anything but show up and work to keep your job."

She glared at him but said nothing.

"I'm sorry. I won't do this again. It's what you said. There's this attraction." He turned toward the window. "I was right the other night. We probably shouldn't see each other, shouldn't even be within ten—no, twenty—feet of each other." He turned toward Persy.

"I agree," Persy said. "Good bye, Jordan . . . I mean, Mr. Prince."

A few minutes later, Jordan called Martha to resume the dictation.

"Excuse me, sir," Martha said primly. "You seem to have something on your cheek."

Jordan took a tissue and wiped it off. He sniffed it and recognized the scent. It was the cream Persy had on her nose. He wadded the tissue up and threw it away.

Chapter Four

"My, Agatha, you've done it again with your special meatloaf." Persy finished the last bite of dinner.

"Thank you. Now, tell me how this thing with the hotel is going."

"Not at all well. We tried communicating with the chain's lawyers but that hasn't gone anywhere. We may try something else but I don't know how much the employees want to risk."

"You mean a strike?" Agatha asked.

"I don't know if it's worth that, but . . . well, we're going to have to think about it. Really need to have another community meeting."

"By the way," Agatha stated as Persy began to clear the table, "a package came for you today."

"Oh?" Persy paused as she scraped food into the garbage. "From who?"

"How would I know? I don't snoop." Agatha stood to leave the kitchen. "It's from your mother."

"Oh, great. I wonder what she's sent this time."

"She sends lovely gifts." Agatha disappeared for a moment and returned with a large box. "Want me to open it?"

"Yes, please." Persy plunged her hands into the soapy water and began washing dishes.

"You could show a little gratitude."

"Yes, I could, but Mother always sends me gifts I don't want because she's trying to get me to do what she wants me to do—which is not what I want to do." Persy scrubbed the plate long after the food was gone.

"Oh, look at this." Agatha lifted a gray pinstriped suit out of the box. She draped it across a chair and unwrapped a mauve blouse from the paper. "Isn't that beautiful? That tiny little skirt—it'll look lovely on you."

"Thanks, Agatha. Now, pack it back up again. I'll give it to the community clothes closet."

"That's smart. You're so tiny, no one else in the neighborhood could wear this, except maybe Susan's twelve year old. Make a real hit at her middle school. Maybe some pearls with it. Of course, with her tennis shoes—"

"Oh, all right, Agatha. I'll stick it in my closet in case I have a chance to wear it or find someone who could use it."

"Look at that lining." Agatha ran her hand across the satin inside the jacket. "Your mother always buys the best."

"And it's wasted on me." Persy opened the sink to let the water run out before she came to the table with a cloth to wipe it. "It looks like something a corporate lawyer would wear and that's what she wants me to be."

"What's wrong with that?"

"I don't want to be a corporate lawyer. She knows that, but she's so darned passive-aggressive."

"Tut, tut. Showing off your education doesn't impress me, missy."

"I know, Agatha. It's not your problem. It's mine." Persy finished wiping the table, rinsed the rag in the sink and dried her hands. "I'll hang it up. Does that make you happy?"

Agatha snorted.

"Puleeeze, won't you love me tonight?" The plaintive notes and mispronounced syllables of a tenor came from the lounge. Persy's back was sore and her head throbbed. The good news and the bad news was that she had to work another shift. She needed the money but twelve hours of dealing was more than she could take with a smile. Still, she attempted to grin at the gambler studying his cards. "Are you going to stay?" she asked in a cheerful voice. He had a ten showing.

"Nah, hit me."

Persy gave him a four.

"Damn, I'm over." The man turned over an eight. "If I didn't have bad luck, I wouldn't have any luck at all."

Maybe you need to learn to play the game, Persy thought as she pushed the cards down the chute. She pulled another card and placed it in front of the next gambler. She was calling for bets when her eye was caught by a shimmering light. She turned and saw the most beautiful woman she'd ever seen: tall, pale blond hair dressed perfectly, a gorgeous face set in lines of adoration as she gazed up at her escort. The shimmering light emanated from the woman's breathtaking dress, covered with silver beads that reflected the light of the chandeliers.

Fascinated by the woman, Persy turned, curious to see what kind of man basked in the admiration of this glorious creature.

My gosh, it was Jordan Prince.

He looked like a prince in his tux. Its lines accented his slim, elegant body. Persy caught her breath as she remembered the warmth of that body against hers. Tonight boredom showed in the dashing lines of his face. The blond turned to him, giving him a brilliant smile while intimately rubbing her finger along his jaw. He took her hand and held it down at his side.

"Hey, dealer, are we going to play here or watch the fashion show?"

"I'm sorry." Persy shook herself and began dealing. How, she thought, did I ever think he'd be interested in me in any way but the physical? Look at the type of woman who hangs on him. That's the type of woman a Prince would date. But what do I care? "You have a seven up. Do you want to stay?" Persy forced herself to think of the game. She looked at the clock. Only another hour and she could get out of here and try to forget the picture of Jordan and that beautiful woman.

Jordan surveyed the casino with a professional eye. It was the most lucrative area of the hotel, and he visited it often.

"Jordan." Gretchen did that annoying thing she did of touching his face. "Isn't it time to go? I told Mother we'd be at the charity ball before ten. It's almost eleven!"

"Yes, Gretchen, I know. You also insisted on that endless meal in the Crown Room when you knew I had to come here before we left. We'll go shortly." As his gaze moved across the tables, they stopped at the sight of a fluffy blond head. *Lord*, he thought, *it can't be Persy still working.* He motioned toward the floor supervisor. "How long has Miss Marsh been dealing?"

"She had a shift from noon to four. Stanley called in sick and she took his four-to-midnight shift."

With her lifeguarding duties this morning, she'd worked a seventeen-hour day. *And she's still smiling. How can she do it? Why does she do it?* He thought back to the woman he'd met at her house. Did she support Agatha too?

And why did he care? He ran his hand through his hair, a gesture he had outgrown except in times of deep study or confusion.

"Oh, Jordan, you've messed up your hair. Let me fix it." Gretchen carefully patted the strands down.

"For heaven's sake, Gretch, you're not my mother. If you find it hideous, I'll go comb it."

"Oh, darling, how could I ever find you hideous?" She giggled.

Jordan hated that. A grown woman who giggled. He observed Persy again. She reached a hand to her neck and surreptitiously attempted to rub it. He saw a frown between her eyes. She closed them and tilted her head back.

She's in pain but she keeps on going. What am I

going to do with her? Why am I wondering that? We aren't even going to see each other again.

Persy opened the brown bag as she and Maria prepared to eat lunch in the employees' lounge. She looked at a peanut butter and jelly sandwich. Why would Agatha give her that? She knew Persy hated peanut butter and jelly.

"I can't eat this." Persy wrapped it again and tossed it in the trash. "What am I going to do for lunch?" She reached into her pocket and pulled out a wrinkled bill. "I guess I'll see if I can talk Hogan into getting me a hamburger for this."

"Don't let the big boss hear you," Maria whispered.

Persy looked up as Jordan crossed the small room. She drew her breath in and felt a tightening in her stomach. It was the second time she'd seen Jordan at the hotel since they'd started . . . oh, what was it they'd started? Since they'd kissed.

But he refused to make eye contact with her. He walked by, turned toward them and nodded. "Good morning, ladies," he said in a calm, deep voice.

"Good morning, sir," Maria said.

"Hello, Jordan." Persy winked at him.

He ignored her.

"Frank, you've got the right idea, but you forgot that the square of . . ." A knock on the door of the house interrupted Persy's efforts to tutor Frank in trig. "Come in," she shouted.

The door opened and Jordan stood there. "Isn't it dangerous to leave your door unlocked?"

Persy was so surprised to see him, she couldn't say a word.

"I didn't think I'd ever see you speechless."

"No, I don't worry about my neighbors in El Valle harming me," Persy stood as she answered his question. "I do lock it at night. What I worry about most is the place the employees cross between the hotel and El Valle. Do you know that outside gangs have been hanging around there for a week, scouting the place?" Persy walked over to the door and leaned against it so Jordan couldn't enter.

"I may have heard that but I don't think it means anything."

"Frank and some of the other young men are getting together a group to patrol that area at night, to keep us safe during shift changes."

"May I come in?"

"Why are you here?"

"How cordial. Not even a 'How nice to see you?' " He ran his hand through his hair before adding, "I don't know. I wanted to see you." As Persy opened her mouth, he held up his hand. "I know, I know. I said we shouldn't but I couldn't help it."

"Well, you had no problem ignoring me at lunch today. You walked right past me as if you'd never seen me before."

"I'm sorry. I didn't know how to react. I wasn't trying to cut you or hurt you. It was a surprise to see you and I wasn't prepared." He looked down at her again. "I came to apologize for that and because you looked so exhausted the other night . . ."

"I know, not nearly as beautiful as your date."

"Ah, you noticed Gretchen. You sound a little jealous."

"No, of course not. I was really tired and she looked so gorgeous. I was envious of how good she looked and how terrible I felt." She opened the door. "Come on in for a minute."

Jordan went to the kitchen table. "What are you working on?" He picked up Frank's textbook.

"This is Frank Moreno." The two men shook hands. "Frank's starting community college. He's having trouble with trig."

"Trig? You're tutoring him in trig?"

"You believe a dog walker shouldn't know trig?" Persy bristled.

"Not at all. I mean there aren't a lot of people who know trig."

"Frank, finish the problems on that page. I need to talk to Mr. Prince. I'll be back in a few minutes."

Barbarella followed them out of the house, purring happily.

Once they were on the porch, Persy turned toward Jordan. "Okay. Why are you here?"

"I don't know." He took her hands and pulled her toward the swing to sit next to him. Barbarella settled herself happily on his foot. "I thought what I felt for you was completely physical but it isn't. I saw how tired you looked after dealing almost twelve hours and it worried me. I wanted to do something to help you, but I have no idea what."

"How did you know I was dealing that long?"

"I asked. I can do that. I'm the boss." He put his arm around her. "I don't know why I did it. I usually don't really care much about other people. I'm not like you."

"What do you mean?" she eyes him suspiciously.

"You obviously care about other people."

"Is that a problem?" Persy asked challengingly.

"Don't get upset, Persy. It's a compliment. I'm not used to people like you. Anytime I see you, there are people all over the place and you love helping them. Frank, with his trig. Agatha. Even what's her name with the grubby little boy from the pancake place. You go out of your way to help others. I wouldn't do that. Sometimes, I admire that."

"Thank you."

Jordan nuzzled her curls and kissed her ear. Persy's emotions were churning. They were too different, she knew. There was no future. This was another one of her disastrous relationships. But when he kissed her, all reason left her. When he was close, she only wanted him closer. She steeled herself. "Not tonight. Perhaps another evening, when we have some idea of where this thing is going."

"Oh, that's how you describe what's happening between us? 'This thing?' "

"Sometimes."

They sat in silence for a few minutes until Jordan asked, "You're not going to let me help you, are you?"

"No, but please don't take that the wrong way. I appreciate your consideration and the offer. I'm pretty independent."

"As if I didn't know." Jordan stood. "Kiss me goodnight?"

In answer, Persy put her arms around his neck and fit her body into his.

After Jordan had returned to the hotel and Frank had finished his trig and left, Agatha came into the living room. "Okay, young lady, there's something I need to know. I mean, the whole story."

"What do you mean?" Persy went into the kitchen for a glass of milk.

"I know you don't much like your mother and I've been patient, but now I want to know why you're here."

"Because I rented the house."

"No, I mean why are you *here*, in El Valle. You're not like us. Why did you come here?"

Persy poured the milk and sat down at the table. "This is the place I want to be, where I choose to be."

"Good start." Agatha settled across from Persy at the table. "But why?"

"It's a long story. Why do you want to know now?"

"Curious. I see you and that Jordan together. Makes me realize how much more you are like him than like us."

"Okay. My parents were fairly well-off . . ."

"They're rich and you live in El Valle now? Did they lose all their money?"

"No, be patient. My mother wanted to be accepted in high society and did everything she could to break in. She even used her own children to try to become important. We were all expected to be perfect in every way: top grades, good athletes, everything."

"So you were Little Miss Perfect."

"Yeah, but it wasn't easy. I worked hard, graduated from college first in my class and became a lawyer, but that wasn't enough for my mother. I realized, finally, that no matter what I did, it would never be good enough for her so why keep trying? I had to do what was best for me. I wanted to be a community organizer, so here I am."

Agatha snorted. "Not all that interesting. I'd sort of hoped you had a few juicy secrets in your past."

"Sorry to disappoint you." Persy drank the rest of her milk and stood while Agatha went back to her bedroom.

Persy watched her go, then went out and sat on the porch swing, looking up at the Gulf Prince Hotel.

An enormous neon sign lit the night sky, flashing shades of purple and green and red. Eighteen stories of white stucco were bathed in the light from a dozen spotlights. In the penthouse of the hotel lived a man who was making her examine herself and her options.

Yes, his kiss aroused her like no man's ever had, but it was his offer of help, his show of concern—so unusual for him she had suspected even before he told her it wasn't like him—that had weakened her. The attraction she felt for him made her incapable of resisting his kiss but it was his consideration for her that almost undid her resolve.

He said he was worried about her. He sounded sincere. He'd checked on her work hours and that showed her another side of him, a gentle, caring side that she liked, as if another person had peeked through that stiff exterior. She feared that the softer, caring aspect of Jordan could make her want to leave the world she'd created in El Valle, could make her want to enter Jordan's world, so like the one she'd left behind.

She thought of the person she'd been until she made that difficult decision three years earlier—nervous, anxious, depressed, unhappy. She called that person Mary Persistence, the name her mother called her, the name she'd used until she was twenty-two. After she threw off the stifling expectations she'd accepted for so long, she'd discovered she was someone else completely: Persy, a person she liked, crazy as she seemed at times.

Could she still be herself—the self she'd become—with Jordan Prince? Was being alone for the rest of her life the only way to preserve who she was?

Chapter Five

"A meal for thirty in the small conference room."
Hogan, chief of catering, made a check on his clipboard. "Persy, you're in charge. Smitty and Maria are working with you. Don't forget, guys, that's the room with the broken swinging door. Show Smitty how it works, Pers? He's new."

"Sure, Hogan. What time will the food be coming up the dumbwaiter?"

"They're to eat at noon so salads will be up in plenty of time before that. The entree will be there shortly after twelve, hot and delicious."

Persy picked up the tablecloths and napkins and led the others onto the service elevator. Once on the third floor, they rushed to get the six tables set, then went into the serving pantry for glasses, ice, and condiments.

"Let me tell you about this crazy door," Persy said to Smitty, motioning toward the swinging door between the pantry and the conference room. "Don't push it out very far, because if you do it springs closed and hits you in the face. Push it about halfway open and slide through or you'll be sorry. Try it."

Smitty gave the door a shove, watched the spring catch and sling the door back at him before he leaped away. "Wow, that could make a real mess."

"Why don't they fix it?" Maria asked.

"We've requested that but management tells us it isn't cost-effective." Persy turned back toward the conference room. "Okay, let's get busy."

Shortly before noon, the meeting in the adjoining conference room had adjourned and people were entering the dining area. Persy and Maria had placed the salad plates at each place, Smitty had served the drinks, but still the food hadn't arrived on the dumbwaiter.

"Looks great so far," Persy said after the last glass of iced tea had been poured, "but the entrees should be here by now." She picked up the phone and called the kitchen. "Hogan, where are the entrees?"

"We had a problem here, Pers. The gravy burned. What's chicken fried steak and mashed potatoes without gravy?"

"Much better for your heart—if you have to eat fried food. When will it be up?"

"Not much longer."

A few minutes later, the salad plates were removed from the tables, glasses refilled, but still no entrees had arrived.

"Where's the food?" Jordan's voice came from the hall.

Persy turned to see him standing in the doorway of the serving area. He looked wonderful and *way* out of her reach in a beautifully tailored pale-gray Italian suit. The shirt was a lovely shade of apricot with a gray and apricot tie. He even managed to make apricot look really macho.

"I don't know. I've called about it. Hogan said it would be right up." At that moment, the first trays appeared on the dumbwaiter.

"I'll get these started before the guests have to wait much longer. Move it, people!" He picked up a tray.

"Be careful," Persy warned as she picked up the second tray. "That door's tricky."

"I think I can go through a door without your help, Persy." Jordan pushed the door wide. As soon as he did, the spring caught and slammed the door shut against him. The tray tilted upward and mashed potatoes and gravy suddenly covered his face and chest. A chicken fried steak landed on his perfectly styled hair, the gravy dipping in rivulets down his face and onto that lovely shirt. Maria and Smitty ran over to see if they could help, biting their lips to keep from laughing.

"Yes, sir, I'm sure you can in most cases." Persy spoke in a quivering voice as she removed the meat from his head and dropped it on a tray. "But this one is a little tricky." She bit her lips but couldn't contain her laugh. "Perhaps I should call for six more dinners?"

"That would be an excellent idea." Jordan handed the tray to Smitty. Persy carefully wiped his eyes with a napkin. "I'm sure you can handle this without me." He turned away, feet squishing in expensive, gravy-filled loafers.

"We'll laugh later," Persy said to the waitstaff. "Right

now, we've got to get the dinners served." She grabbed the phone and dialed. "Hogan, we need six more entrees."

"Didn't we count right?"

"Oh, you counted right. You just didn't count on Mr. Prince."

"What?"

"No time! I'll tell you later, but I think you can depend on this door getting repaired soon!" When Persy hung up, she heard a crash in the hallway. Dashing out, she saw Jordan feeling his way toward the elevator, blinded by the potatoes and gravy that dripped down his forehead and into his eyes.

"Hold on, Jordan, let me help you get cleaned up." Persy turned back toward the serving area and shouted over her shoulder. "I'll be back in a minute." She turned back toward Jordan and took her apron off, using it to gently clean his eyes before leading him into the staff restroom. The two of them barely fit in the tiny space.

Persy looked up at him and ran her index finger down Jordan's right cheek, across his chin, and up the left cheek. "Poor man, you've ruined that beautiful suit. Let me help you."

Jordan turned toward the mirror. When he saw himself, he groaned. "Oh, great, exactly what a friend would do." He looked at the line Persy had drawn through the mashed potatoes and gravy. "You drew a smile in this stuff. Why would you make me into a happy face?"

"I'm sorry. I couldn't stop myself. You know how I am."

Jordan took a glob of the mixture from his neck,

contemplated it while he weighed it in his hand, then wiped it across Persy's face. Before she could react, he pulled her against him, rubbing his face on her curls, turning them into a slimy snarl. "There, that makes me feel a little better."

"I can't believe—" she sputtered, looking up at him with wide eyes.

"I'm sorry, Persy, but you know how I am. Uptight and really inhibited. I don't know why I did that but it felt great."

"You jerk! I can't believe you'd—" Persy leaped at him and tried to rub the mess into Jordan's hair, but she was so short that Jordan was able to grab her, lift her off her feet, and hold her away from him while she struggled.

Persy reached for Jordan's chest and grabbed some of the potatoes, which she smacked across his face.

"You wait, Persy. I'll get you. I'm a lot bigger than you." He rescued the mound she'd put on his nose, held Persy with one hand, and looked into her face. In a moment, the teasing turned to desire.

Jordan drew her fiercely against him with one arm and lowered his mouth to hers. He held her against him, his left hand on her back, and moved his right up to her neck to pull her lips against his. As the kiss lengthened, Persy found one of her hands in Jordan's hair, stroking the gluey mess.

He shifted his weight to hold her more comfortably and said, "Wait a minute. My foot's caught in the wastebasket." He shook his foot, attempting to kick the small plastic bin off. "There. Got it." He lowered his mouth again.

Persy rocked back against the wall and her head

exploded with pain. "Ouch!" She tried to lean away from the wall. "I hit my head against the paper towel dispenser."

Jordan again shifted his hold, turned, and lowered Persy slightly. She felt something give behind her as he pushed against her. Instantly, there was the sound of a motor and Persy felt warm air blowing against her back.

"I think we turned on the electric hand dryer." Persy couldn't keep a chuckle out of her voice.

The lunacy of the situation struck them both and they burst into laughter. Jordan let go of Persy and sat on the sink, guffawing until he was out of breath. Persy joined the laughter until tears were rolling down her face and mixing with the potatoes and gravy.

"Look at us!" Persy turned toward the mirror. The two were covered with a greasy white mixture that obscured their features and clothes and pulled their hair into spikes. "We look terrible. Are there enough paper towels to clean up this mess?"

"Come down to my suite. We can wash up down there. I have lots of thick towels and clean clothes."

"No, thanks! I have to get back to work. But, how can I when I look like this? You go on, I'll take care of myself here. How I'll explain this to Smitty and Maria, I don't know."

"I'll send up a towel and clean shirt." Jordan went to the door, then turned around and grinned. "Persy, when I'm with you, I do the most inappropriate things. You definitely are a bad influence!"

*　*　*

"Darn it!" Jordan shouted as he attempted to put his studs in their tiny holes. He was alone and not very happy about putting his tux on again, but he'd promised his mother. Tonight he was to escort Miss Adrienne St. Martin-Bythorpe to the opera when what he really wanted to do—as much as he attempted to deny it—was see Persy again.

In retrospect, he told himself, being covered with mashed potatoes and gravy was really inappropriate, as much fun as it had seemed at the time. But nonetheless, it was unsuitable for the owner of the Prince Hotels. As much as he enjoyed kissing Persy, he reminded himself about his background and his name and what he owed his family, and that did not included frolicking in food with Miss Marsh.

The good thing about Adrienne was that she'd treat him like Lesley Jordan Rutherford Prince instead of a man who'd been kissing a waitress in the restroom and enjoying it tremendously.

So there! With a final shove, he got the last stud in place and admired his reflection in the mirror. Ambivalence had no place in the character of a Prince.

But, in a back corner of his brain that he tried to close off, he wished he were seeing Persy tonight.

"Now, this is the way the things work," Tony Rufino explained. "You slip the mask on over your head and when you pull the string on the side, the eyes fall out. Got it?"

"Yes, I think I can handle it." Persy looked at the hideous creation. She shivered from the draft in the enormous Rufino Brothers' Warehouse, filled with costumes and novelties. "Why do you want me to sell these in front of the opera house?"

"Because, kid, these are Phantom of the Opera masks, get it? So you sell them in front of the opera, okay? Now, here's your costume."

Persy looked at the handful of material he gave her. She held it up in front of her and realized it barely covered her chest and was cut to show as much thigh as possible. "I'm not going to wear this."

"What do you mean? You wear that or no job."

"What I mean is, this costume doesn't fit your creative idea. You have a phantom mask, so I should wear a phantom costume. The highbrow crowd that goes to the opera won't buy from a hussy with no clothes on. These are discriminating people who will appreciate an entire package—mask *and* costume."

"Hey, that's great. Where would I find a phantom costume?"

"Leave it to me," Persy said with relief. "I'll find something."

The "something" turned out to be a black leotard with tights and a cape that belonged to the Superman costume of Sammy, Susan's youngest son. "Oh, well," Persy studied her reflection. "I do look ridiculous but I'm not going to see anyone I know. If I did, they wouldn't recognize me anyway. I'm wearing a mask."

Persy discovered that people stopped to inspect the mask if she made her pitch funny instead of frightening. She'd stood next to the door of the opera for five minutes without selling a mask. So she made up a song about, "My goog-goog-googelly eyes," and did a silly little dance, at the end of which she pulled the string and the eyes fell out. To her delight, this was greeted with laughter and sales.

Persy had just started her song when she looked up and saw Jordan with another long-legged beauty. He helped her from a limo, then stood and held his arm out to her. A clone of the other women, Persy thought, except this one was a redhead. Her lovely skin showed almost to her navel in her sequined dress with low décolleté.

Persy froze. He wouldn't recognize her dressed like this, she hoped, but decided to turn toward the wall to make sure.

"Hey, girlie," a man in the crowd shouted, "let's see that bump and grind again."

Before she turned around, Persy realized his loud voice would distract Jordan from the redhead, but she was sure he wouldn't recognize her. She turned her back to the crowd and began the goog-goog-googelly eye song in a high, tinny voice.

"Persy?"

"Well, hi!" Persy turned to face Jordan, plastering a fake grin on her face. "You must be going to the opera," she said inanely.

"Another part-time job?"

"No, actually, a career change. I've always been dedicated to the arts."

"Who is this lovely creature?" The redhead said as she took a possessive hold on Jordan's arm.

"Adrienne, this is Persy Marsh. Persy, Adrienne St. Martin-Bythorpe."

"Persy, what a lovely name." Sugary sarcasm dripped from her words. "Is that short for something?"

"Yes, it is." Persy nodded to Adrienne. "It certainly

is a pleasure to meet you. Jordan, I need to get back to work." As Persy attempted to maintain her façade of normalcy, Jordan reached to examine the string, pulled it, and both eyes fell out, swinging back and forth on long springs in front of her. "Oh, darn!" she whispered. Jordan's lips quivered as he attempted not to laugh. He turned to escort the poised and glamorous Adrienne toward the door of the opera house.

"What an interesting young woman," Persy heard Adrienne say. "How ever did you meet her?"

Jordan turned back. "How much are those things?"

"Ten dollars."

"Are you working on commission?"

"Yes."

"Okay, let me have ten of them."

"What in the world are you going to do with ten of these things?"

"I have friends . . ."

"I'm sure it's exactly what people in your circle wear."

"That's not entirely true, but I know Frank would love them. I'm sure I can think of others." He handed Persy a hundred-dollar bill.

"Thank you." Persy gracefully accepted the money. "Will you take them with you, or do you want me to deliver them tomorrow?"

"Can you bring them to my office? All except one mask. I'll take that with me. I may feel an urge to sing about goog-goog-googelly eyes—is that an Andrew Lloyd Webber song?—and would hate not to have the mask."

"Okay, here's one. I'll deliver the others."

"It's Thursday. Shouldn't you be tutoring Frank tonight?"

"I leave once the opera starts."

"Fine. Well, good evening, Miss Marsh."

"Mr. Prince." She turned back to the crowd and began to sing again.

"I have a delivery for Mr. Prince, Martha." Persy entered the receptionist's office and rested her full arms on the desk.

"He expects you, Miss Marsh. I'll buzz him but you can go on in."

Persy gathered her courage and went.

"Here're your masks." She pushed the door open with a free hand while the stack of masks tilted. "Where do you want them?"

"Oh, here on my desk." Jordan leaned back in his chair and pointed at the corner of the desk. "I want them close at hand. You never know when I may want to give one to someone."

"A gift from the Prince Hotel chain. It certainly fits your image." Persy placed a few on the cleared space. "Tell me, how in the world did you recognize me in that absurd costume with my back to you."

"I have found certain parts of you very memorable, Persy. Do you want to know more?"

She dropped the rest of the stack. "No, that's enough." A flush started up her neck. "Thank you for buying the masks."

"You're welcome. I'm sure I'll use them."

"You know you won't. You wanted to help me out. I appreciate that."

"Don't make me into a saint. You've already established that I'm not."

"Oh, so you don't want me to show my appreciation?"

"What did you have in mind?" Jordan stood and lazily came around the desk.

"Nothing, really." Persy moved away nervously.

"Don't you owe me something? An apology perhaps? After all, you laughed at me when I was all covered with gravy. How do you expect to keep working here if you laugh at the boss?"

"I'm hardworking and work cheap. I know it was rude but it was so . . ." Struggling not to laugh again, Persy took a deep breath. "Really, really funny! But I shouldn't have done it, even though it was funny."

"Some women seem to find me irresistible and throw themselves at me. There's only one who laughs at me."

She grinned at him but didn't laugh.

He studied her. Her eyelashes, thick and long, fanned across her cheeks. She was the most beautiful woman he'd ever seen. Oh, not classically beautiful. It was the light of her personality that made her features glow, but he couldn't tell her that. It gave away feelings that he still struggled with. Instead, he put his arms around her and touched her lips lightly and unhurriedly, delighting in the sharp intake of her breath.

When she finally broke the embrace, she looked up at him. "Why do we get along so well physically but are so different in all the ways that matter?"

"I think this one matters." Jordan feathered kisses down her neck.

"But we're so different."

"Maybe we aren't all that different," he said, refusing to let her move away. "Maybe people can change."

"Can Princes change? I thought royalty was always sure that they were right."

"I think if he wanted to, a Prince could change. But I know a rebellious hellcat who always seems to believe she's right, too. Can a curly-headed blond community reformer change?"

"I don't know. I don't even know if she recognizes the need to do that."

"Let's go out to dinner tonight and talk about it."

"I can't tonight. I have a meeting. Tomorrow night?"

"Great."

"Don't forget."

There wasn't a chance in the world he would.

Chapter Six

"Will the meeting please come to order?" Persy looked around her at the people filling the chairs and jammed into the corners in the church basement. The hall was bursting with employees of the Gulf Prince and their families.

"The purpose of our meeting tonight is to decide the next step to take about the thoroughfare between the hotel and El Valle. As you know, we've discussed this with the legal department of the Prince Hotels but have gotten nowhere. The position of the Prince Hotel chain is that such modifications are not cost-effective and that there is no danger to the employees. The floor is open for discussion." Before Persy finished her last sentence, hands were waving in the air.

"Persy, I'd like to speak." An elderly woman on the front row stood.

"Yes, Mrs. Matthews. The chair recognizes you."

"Persy, you know my family's been working at the hotel for years. We owe the hotel a lot but I think they owe me something too. I was robbed two months ago coming across that dark path when I took my son his dinner. I lost fifty dollars. That's the money I was going to give my grandson to rent a tux for his prom. It meant a lot to both of us. The hotel says I was trespassing because I haven't worked there for years. The police can't find the men that robbed me so I'm out fifty dollars. The worst part is, I'm scared for anyone to pass through there in the dark and those that run that big hotel don't care."

Voices shouted agreement. Other speeches followed, most agreeing with Mrs. Matthews.

"I know you're all angry, but what do we do?" Persy asked finally.

"I think you should meet with Mr. Prince, Persy," a tall man in the back suggested. "You're a smart lawyer. Can't you talk to him and explain what we want? It's not much."

"Brownie, I'm not sure I'm the most effective spokesperson."

"Yes, Persy, you are!" Brownie's wife stood up. "You're smart and you aren't afraid of anything or anybody!"

"I think we should strike!" Mrs. Matthews spoke again.

"Do you think this is worth threatening a strike?"

A low rumble passed through the crowd.

"No, I'd rather work something out," a woman sitting in the back row said. "But if we say absolutely we won't strike, we don't have a threat. Maybe we don't want to say absolutely no to anything."

"Tell 'em we're willing to cooperate. I'll do some of the work." Frank stood up. "I tried to cut the bushes down right after Mrs. Matthews was robbed but the security guys kicked me off the property."

"What you're saying is that we want to work something out. We're willing to provide labor if the hotel will put in the lights?" Persy asked. "Is that the consensus of the meeting?"

The heads nodded and voices agreed.

"Go to it, Persy!"

"Will someone please make a motion?"

"I move that Persy represent us about the pathway," Mrs. Matthews said.

"Second," said several people in unison.

"All in favor?" Persy asked. Voices shouted "Aye!"

"All opposed?" When there was silence, Persy said, "The motion passes unanimously."

Persy dressed with special care the next evening, then cursed at herself in the mirror.

"What's the matter?" Agatha stood at the door of Persy's bedroom. "I think you look real pretty."

Persy looked at her reflection. She wore a long white skirt, a silky red top with tiny straps, and red sandals.

"That's the problem. I still care how people think I look! I thought I was over that! I promised myself that when I changed my lifestyle, I'd be myself and forget what other people thought. Now I find that I want Jordan to think I look terrific."

"So, what's wrong with wanting to look beautiful for the man you love? I always dress up special for Burt on bingo nights."

"I don't love Jordan! I don't! I don't! I don't!" She

began to wipe her lipstick and mascara off. "I don't want to put on makeup and be artificial."

"Young lady, that's what I call a tantrum. Why is it so important that you not fall in love with Jordan Prince? If you don't want to, why keep seeing him?" Agatha entered and sat on the bed.

"I don't know." Persy threw herself in a heap on the bed. "This is the most confusing thing that ever happened to me. He's everything I don't like in a person. He's rich and doesn't use that money to help people. He doesn't have much of a sense of humor, although I think it's improving. He doesn't believe in recycling! His whole philosophy is completely different from mine and I know this is only leading to heartbreak and pain, but when I'm with him, I forget that." She dropped her brush. "I should never, ever see him again but I forget that when I see him. There are times he is very sweet, even thoughtful, when he seems to care for me as a person and that's really hard to resist. Oh, Agatha, I'm so happy and I'm so miserable!" She put her hand on Agatha's arm.

Agatha's stiff posture didn't relax. Uncomfortable, she patted Persy on the back and said, "There, there," as she pushed away from Persy. "Don't worry about it. You've chosen to see what happens, and I think that's wise. If you broke off now you'd never know if things could work out, if one or both of you could change."

"But why would I have to change? I'm not uptight like Jordan." Persy lay back against her pillow.

"I think you might need to realize lots of what you think is Jordan's problem may be yours. It might could be that you can't accept a rich person. I mean, the fact that he likes nice things doesn't mean he's a terrible person."

"There are people in El Valle who could feed their families with what he spends on clothing."

"That's right, but that's your priority for money, not his. His family has made the money. Certainly he should be able to spend some of it on himself."

"But, Agatha, he spends all of it on himself! And his clothes and car and his gorgeous women."

"Perhaps he needs someone to help him understand better ways to spend his money."

"Oh."

"Could be he's never met anyone with different priorities."

"Do you think?"

"Maybe you're exactly what he needs to show him the way, but you're not going to do it with your makeup running and your eyes red from where you've scrubbed off your mascara."

"Thank you, Agatha. You make me feel much better. I'll think of this as a mission, converting the power of the Prince to the use of the common folk." Persy smiled. "Maybe I'll have fun at the same time." She stood, went to her dressing table, and powdered her nose.

"Oh, Jordan, what a lovely restaurant." She turned and looked around her. "There's even a pianist."

He seated her as the hostess handed Persy a menu, then watched as she started to play with the flowers in the center of the table. Would she weave another wreath?

"Why don't you look at the menu?"

She dropped her fingers and smiled at him. "Well done. That's what's known as redirecting."

"What is?" Jordan looked at Persy over the top of his menu.

"In psychological circles, when you want to stop a person from an action that manifests a mental illness, you redirect that person. For instance, if an aggressive person is losing control, you sing with him or take him for a walk or ask him to recite the steps to control aggression. In society, we call it changing the subject, but I believe you were redirecting me."

Jordan looked puzzled. "Where did you learn that?"

"In school. I'm not an illiterate boob, you know."

"I never thought that, but I guess I never thought how much education you might have. Where did you go to school?"

"Stanford."

"Stanford! You must have a very good brain."

"Well, yes, I do." She studied the menu attentively while Jordan waited for her to continue. "I think I'll have the strip steak. I'm so tired of chicken. We have it so often because it's cheap and good for you. Is the steak good here?"

"Yes. How long did you go to Stanford?"

"Oh, until I finished. Would you like to share an appetizer? They have deluxe nachos that sound wonderful."

"What did you major in?"

"Pre-law. Can I have wine also?"

"How do you know psychology?"

"Law isn't the only thing I studied. I worked one summer in a mental hospital and remember some of the stuff."

"You worked in a mental hospital?"

"I think I'd like white wine. I know that isn't the right thing to have with red meat. Do you mind?"

"No, of course, whatever." Jordan perused the menu as the waitress took their order. That finished, he asked, "Are you a lawyer?"

"Do I look like a lawyer? Are there a lot of lawyers who deal in your casino? Who walk dogs? Have you seen any other lawyers with googelly eyes?"

"Yes, to the last. You still haven't answered my question. Are you a lawyer?"

"Maybe, and that's the only answer you're going to get. What are you having?"

"Why do you refuse to tell me anything about yourself? I'm not prying. I'm just interested."

"Because I'm not that person who went to college and did all that stuff. I'm uncomfortable talking about it because I'm different. I want people to like me for who I *am* not, who I was. I want to enjoy now. With you."

The food appeared and they both ate quietly. At the end of the meal, Persy sipped her decaf while Jordan enjoyed his Irish coffee.

"Have you ever had trouble walking a dog you couldn't control?" Jordan leaned toward Persy.

"No, why?"

"You're a tiny person. I bet some of those dogs weigh as much as you do."

"It doesn't matter how much they weigh. They have to know who's in charge."

"So you let them know immediately that you're the boss." Jordan laughed. "That sounds like you. You never worry that one won't listen to you? I can see you being pulled at top speed around the parking lot by an out-of-control mastiff."

"Never! It wouldn't dare!" Persy laughed at herself, then became serious. "There is one thing I am really worried about: that entrance to the parking lot that we have to go through to get to the hotel. If anyone were to get hurt, they'd have a good case against the hotel."

"Come on, Persy, let's not talk about that. We've discussed this with our lawyers and insurance company and feel we're okay."

"It wouldn't take a lot. Only trimming the bushes back and installing some lighting."

"You certainly know how to ruin a great evening. Okay, if you insist on talking about this, I'll explain." He leaned back in his chair with a sigh. "What you don't realize is how much money it would cost. There are no electric lines there. The parking lot is lit from lights close to the hotel. To keep the aesthetic value, we'd have to put the lines underground. That means tearing up the parking lot, which means our guests would be inconvenienced by the lack of parking and the noise. If we have fewer guests, we have to lay off staff. In addition, we'd have to repave, which costs money. The lights are not inexpensive, either."

"You could tear up the parking lot bit by bit, and not inconvenience guests. Yes, it would cost money. On the other hand, think how you'd feel if anyone got hurt there, or killed, because you didn't take precautions. That kind of publicity wouldn't be good for the hotel either."

"I wouldn't like that to happen, but we had a study done. The consultants have assured us there's little danger."

"How much did those consultants cost you? A bundle, I bet. You could have spent that money on the improvements."

Jordan continued as if she hadn't said anything. "The consultants suggest that if you employees would walk in groups, you'd feel safer."

"We can't always. Sometimes Susan has a sick child and has to come back on her break to check on him. Sometimes I have odd hours and no one's going over or coming home. Occasionally, on a late or early shift, we have to walk alone. Besides, we're not kids who need to buddy up. We're adults asking our employer to make conditions at the hotel safer."

"Persy, it wouldn't be cost-effective. That's the bottom line. It would cost us more to install the lights and keep the bushes trimmed back than it's worth."

"I think one of your employees' pain and suffering would be worth something to you."

"I don't think it's going to come to that."

"You are so selfish!"

"And you're always right on your crusades. I don't know why I want to be with you. You're the most aggravating . . ."

"No, you are! You'd try the patience of a saint."

"You're far from a saint, Persy. You don't run the hotel and take all the financial risks, but you want to decide how we should spend our money. Stay out of that. It isn't your business."

"Yes," Persy stood and leaned over him, "the health and safety of the people who live in El Valle *are* my business and it should be yours, too."

"Persy, sit down and be good."

"Don't put me down! I'm not being bad. I'm discussing something I'm very concerned about."

"In a loud voice, in a crowded restaurant. People are staring at us."

"Let them look. I don't care what they think." Persy pushed her chair back and tossed her napkin on the table. "Don't bother to take me home. I can find the way. I'd hate to make you do anything that isn't cost-effective."

As she stood, her glance fell on her glass of ice water. She eyed it, then looked up at Jordan.

"Persy, that's not a good idea."

"Why not?" But she couldn't. It was immature. Drawing herself up to her full five feet, she stomped away from the table.

"Persy . . ." She heard his voice as she dashed out the door. How in the world was she going to get home? She turned to go back inside to call Frank but ran into Jordan's chest.

"What has gotten into you? We were having a nice dinner together before you went off."

"I'm sorry." She suddenly felt deflated and angry with herself. "I have a terrible temper and when I'm mad, I do dumb things."

He didn't say a word but she knew he wanted to.

"I wasn't at all professional. I shouldn't have brought up the pathway at dinner. I should have waited to meet with you on it." She shook her head.

"Persy, are you a lawyer?"

"Yes, but not a very good one."

He took her hand and led her to a bench in front of the restaurant. "Why not?"

"Isn't it obvious? I get so passionately involved in

my cases I can't do a good job. A lawyer has to remain objective and in control." She shrugged as she sat. "You may have noticed I don't."

"Yes, that did jump out at me. I admire your passion. You care deeply for people."

Persy nodded and looked up at Jordan. He studied her face, as if searching for something there. What?

"I admire that. I'm not used to being with someone who cares about something other than the bottom line."

"Oh? But your family—"

"Oh, personally my family cares about all of us, but professionally, we're very business-oriented. We don't allow our emotions to take over." He shook his head. "You have me wondering if that's always the right way to approach everything."

"Sometime, could we discuss my concerns? I promise to be very professional, if it kills me."

"Call Martha and set up a meeting. Now, let me go in and take care of the bill. After that, why don't you and I take a stroll across the beach before I take you home?"

"I'm still hungry. Could we grab a hamburger someplace?"

The next morning, Persy shivered as she walked through the dark pathway—partly from fear, but mostly because it was still a little chilly and dark. Although, once through the dense bushes, she could look toward the horizon and see tinges of light.

What an idiot, she thought. I'll probably freeze from swimming so early but it's better than running into . . . oh, anyone I don't want to meet.

But she wasn't even kidding herself. She was avoiding Jordan and came to swim at five-thirty because the pampered scion of the Prince family wouldn't be there at that hour. She was still embarrassed about her outburst two evenings earlier and worried about what she would say when she met with him at two o'clock that afternoon.

After arriving at the pool, slipping off her sandals, and tossing her towel on a chair, Persy dove in. She did two laps quickly, racing back and forth. When she finally woke up and was thinking clearly, she slowed down, taking her time and feeling the relaxing tingling of a good warm-up spread through her. She flipped over to her back for two laps, noticing that the sun was up, and decided to finish up with one more lap.

As she approached the end of the pool, her hand reached for the wall but instead ran into something that seemed softer than the wall and a little furry. She swung her other hand up and hit the same thing. She moved a hand down, felt cloth and stopped. Oh, Lord, no! Persy thought. She dropped her arms and stood.

"Good morning, Persy." Jordan leaned against the end of the pool, arms folded and wearing a delighted smile.

"Oh, darn!" Persy carefully kept her eyes on Jordan's face. "I'm sorry."

"Don't mention it. It certainly woke me up. I hope you've had an . . . invigorating swim." His lips continued to twitch.

"Very nice, thank you. Now, if you'll excuse me?" Persy headed toward the steps.

"Persy?" His voice was soft, questioning, uncertain; his arms, open.

Persy turned back toward him. "Jordan?" She walked the short distance to him, leaving swirls churning in the water, and hopped up the steps and his arms. His lips descended on hers, circling lazily and pulling her into a trance.

She broke away. "Jordan, not here, not now."

"Why not now?" he asked.

"Because." She tried to move away but his arms held her tightly. "Because everyone can see us. Because you and I are opponents on this thing." She gestured toward the pathway.

"You think this might be construed as conflict of interest by our various constituencies?" He whispered against her lips.

"Oh, yes!" Persy pushed away from him and floated backwards. "You know this isn't the time or place."

"I know, but for a moment, I didn't care. To think I used to have self-control." Jordan stood straight against the wall and took a deep breath.

"Why do we always end up kissing? You know, there are times I don't even like you!"

"Oh, I think you do." Jordan grinned with so much satisfaction that Persy longed to slap him.

Persy turned and headed for her bag, attempting to look poised as water ran off her body. She slipped into her shoes and threw the towel around her shoulders. "Good day, Mr. Prince," she said icily, but she didn't feel that way, not even close. "I'll see you this afternoon."

Persy again dressed with special care, wearing black slacks and a white blouse with a black and white scarf

Agatha contributed, and arrived at the office a few minutes early.

After a ten-minute wait, the intercom on Martha's desk beeped and Jordan's voice came through. "Send Miss Marsh in."

"Thank you, Martha." Persy stood, took a deep breath, held it, then exhaled slowly before entering the executive office. "Hello, Mr. Prince. Thank you for seeing me."

Jordan was standing. "Please sit, Miss Marsh." He motioned her toward a chair.

"You are aware, I believe," Persy said as she seated herself, "that I represent the association of employees of the Gulf Prince who live in El Valle and who use the pathway north of the hotel to come to work and return home?"

"Yes. Is this an incorporated association?" Jordan sat and leaned back in his chair.

"No, it is an informal group that meets to improve the conditions in the neighborhood. The association would like to ask you to consider improvements to the thoroughfare between the hotel and La Paloma."

"What are you requesting?" He looked at Persy over templed fingers.

"We'd like adequate lighting . . ." She met his eyes with professional calm.

"What do you consider adequate?"

"We estimate four street lights on posts. We would also like the bushes to be cut back and a sidewalk to be poured."

"Ah, the sidewalk is, I believe a new idea."

"For a distance of fifteen feet, between the parking lot and the street, the employees walk on dirt. When it rains, this is muddy and slippery and could be dangerous."

"I thought you believed the danger was from theft."

"Yes, but, while this area is being improved, we would like the sidewalk to be added."

"What is the association willing to contribute?"

"We will donate labor to cut back the bushes and keep them contained."

"In your scenario, the hotel is to donate the electricity, lights, and installation, as well as pouring this sidewalk?"

"Yes."

"I will consider your request, but there are other alternatives which I suggest you try."

"Legally, I believe we have grounds to use this right of way."

"I don't dispute that. Any employee who lives in El Valle may walk along that path as often as they want, whenever they want. I don't believe the hotel needs to make it into a luxury item. However, I will have the legal staff look into this."

"Darn it, Jordan, you're going to spend more on lawyers than these improvements will cost!" Persy took another deep breath and sat back in her chair. *Play it cool*, she chided herself. *Don't let him see how angry you are.*

"Hardly that. The lawyers, Miss Marsh, are on retainer. We might as well use them since we pay them."

He looked cold, professional, his expression hard and set. There was no hint of the man who'd laughed with her or held her or kissed her.

"I do have a question, Miss Marsh. Why is this

coming up now? Is it because you are in the neighborhood?"

"No, Mr. Prince. The trees and bushes along the
pathway had been fairly small. Almost a year ago,
members of the association tell me, there was addi-
tional privacy landscaping done around the hotel, at
which time large, fast-growing bushes were planted.
At the same time, there was an infestation of trumpet
vines, which took over many of the trees and made
the area very dark. That is when the association became concerned."

"Persy, doggone it, you have to give me some ideas
here, some help. I can't do this just to make you
happy. After all, there have been no incidences of rob-
beries or injuries there."

Persy frowned. "Certainly you know what happened
to Mrs. Matthews. She had fifty dollars stolen from
her and your legal department refused to listen to her."

"Do you mean Hattie Matthews? Who worked at
the hotel for years? Was she hurt?" Jordan leaned for-
ward.

"No, but very frightened and angry."

"I apologize, Persy. I didn't know. Legal never told
me." He thought for a moment. "She lost fifty dollars?
And we didn't reimburse her?"

"No, sir."

"Any other problems?"

"Mitzi Garner fell one evening. She sprained her
ankle and had to wait for someone to help her back
home."

"That could have happened even with the lights."

"But not with the sidewalk. She stepped in a hole—
which she might have been able to see with the lights."

"Thank you for the information, Miss Marsh. I'll look into it, and you can be sure Mrs. Matthews will not lose her money."

"Thank you, Mr. Prince." Persy stood and nodded at him. She didn't reach out to shake hands with him, she was afraid to touch him. "I appreciate your spending time with me."

Persy turned and left Jordan's office, nodded at Martha as she went past her desk, and came into the hallway where Susan waited for her.

"Was it okay?" Susan asked.

"It was difficult." Persy leaned against the wall and took a few deep breaths. "I still don't think he sees the need for this. I hope no one gets hurt because Mr. Prince is so proud."

Chapter Seven

Blue, gray, black, brown. Jordan surveyed his jackets in the closet, divided into sections by color. On a rod beneath his jackets were his trousers: blue, gray, black, brown, white. On the opposite side of his walk-in closet were his shirts: blue, gray, tan, white, pastels.

Below his shirts, his shoes were lined up, each pair perfectly straight, with the tip of the toe on an imaginary line that ran from the back of the closet to the edge of the door. Around the top of the closet were shelves where his sweaters were stacked: blue, gray, black, brown, white, red. On another rod at the end of the closet his suits hung: blue, gray, black, and brown. Next to the suits, formal wear was stored covered and beside them was the glass-fronted cabinet containing his ties.

Jordan selected a blue blazer and shrugged into it, glad he could wear a sports coat to the casual party at the club his mother had manipulated him into that

Wednesday evening. He straightened his blue tie, checked his hair in the mirror, and admired his reflection.

Wouldn't Persy be surprised that he had recommended those changes? He couldn't help but think how she'd react. He'd like to see that wonderful smile again.

Tonight she'd be working from 3:00-11:30 P.M. He'd checked the schedules. He would like to see her again, darn it, but he had this thing at the club.

He had to admit, sometimes Persy presented more of a challenge than he was up to. After all, there were women, many women, who respected and liked and admired and even adored him as he was. Never would they cause a scene in a restaurant. They treasured the time spent with him and valued his opinion. Not one of his previous dates had ever tried to change him. They thought he was perfect exactly the way he was.

Maybe that's why they were so boring.

Persy felt terrible. She'd told everyone she was fine, that she was tough, and laughed off the confrontation with Jordan, but she wasn't fine. She was incredibly tired from trying to do too much. Her face hurt from the grin she wore and her head ached with tension.

She was calling for bets when she saw him. The Prince stood on the top step of the staircase and looked down on his subjects. There was another woman with him, a brunette version of the other two. Where did they come from, all these tall, gorgeous women? They were thin—tennis, diet, and exercise, Persy guessed—but how did they all get so tall? Certainly the rich didn't have a special gene for height, did they? Or, perhaps, the tall, glamorous ones had always staked out Jordan. They would. He'd be perfect for them. He'd give them furs and jewels and they'd have lovely little children to put into private schools and to drive to tennis and violin lessons. Persy blinked back tears— from the smoke, she told herself. Stop mooning over him, she lectured herself, then began dealing from the shoe.

For the third time, she slapped the hand of the drunk who was trying to pinch her. "Is this man bothering you?" the floor boss asked Persy.

"No, I can handle him."

"Mr. Prince said I should throw him out."

Persy's head jerked up. Jordan was watching her from ten feet away. He was furious, she knew. At her or at the man? She didn't care. "Tell him I'm fine. I can take care of myself." Persy resumed dealing.

It was one o'clock in the morning, and the women from the literacy class were just leaving.

"Bye, Persy, thanks." Mrs. Smythe moved past her onto the porch. "You're such a dear having this class after we get off at midnight. Otherwise, we couldn't make it."

"Oh, yes, Persy, thanks," another class member said. "I'm so excited. This week I was able to read a story in one of my son's books!"

"See you next week." Persy stood on the porch and watched the five women move away. She was so pleased the women were learning but these late classes were exhausting.

As she turned back to enter the house, the glistening whiteness of the hotel drew her eyes. The curtains of one of the windows of the penthouse were open and the light outlined someone standing there. Was it Jordan? Probably. Was that woman with him? Why was he looking out the window if he were entertaining the gorgeous brunette?

Of course, he could just be looking out the window, not even looking at her. There was a nice view of the ocean as it curved around the peninsula. She knew because she'd cleaned the suite.

Persy went down the steps and stood in the yard before she lifted her arms over her head and waved. He waved back at her, his hand outlined against the light.

Stop mooning over him! He obviously preferred those society women who clung to him, so why should she care? She went back into the house, throwing herself on the sofa as she tried to force her foolish fantasies about Jordan away.

The evening with Daphne hadn't been successful. He'd been moody and unpleasant. She'd been coquettish and he wasn't up to flirting. Jordan took her home early, then stopped in the hotel lounge for a drink, which he brought up to the suite with him. When he opened the curtains to survey the finger of land and the ocean surrounding it, he noticed a few lights glowing in El Valle, one in Persy's house. As he watched, people came out and went down the block, then someone—it must be Persy, he imagined—stood in the middle of the yard, looked up at his window, and waved. He lifted his arms and motioned back. The figure watched him for a moment before going back into the house.

What's she doing now? Why is she always helping people and wearing herself out? Why can't she go to bed and not spend all her energy on others?

Might as well ask why the sun rises. That was Persy.

Jordan didn't like working Saturday mornings but he had paperwork to catch up on. When he entered the office, the first thing he did was look out at the pool. She wasn't there. He hadn't seen her since the other night when she'd waved at him.

He tried to ignore his disappointment. Gary was lifeguarding this morning. Why should he care who was lifeguarding this morning anyway? He opened a file drawer and saw the pile of masks he'd pushed in there earlier in the week. He should throw them away. Instead, he took the file he wanted and closed the drawer. After he picking up a pencil and a copy of the hotel budget, he studied the papers carefully, crossing through some items, changing numbers. The phone rang ten times before he remembered that Martha wasn't there to pick it up. He hit the answer button and said, "Prince."

"Is this Jordan Prince?"

"Yes."

"Mr. Prince, this is Lorraine Hathaway from KRRP–TV. I've been trying to get in touch with you all morning for your reaction to last night's incident. Can you give me a quote?"

He continued to work on the budget as she talked. "I'm sorry, Miss Hathaway. I'm working in my office and don't know what you're talking about."

"Are you aware of the seriousness of the injuries your employee suffered?"

"What injuries, Miss Hathaway?" Jordan put his pencil down and focused his attention on the phone.

"One of your employees was beaten and robbed in your parking lot early this morning. Didn't you know?"

"No, I didn't." He'd gotten home late. During the entire evening with Daphne, a date he'd made weeks earlier, he'd kept wishing she'd turn into that curly-haired little blond witch. This morning, he'd leaped out of bed, grabbed breakfast, and headed to the office. "When did this happen? What happened?"

"It seems one of your employees—a Persy Marsh. Is that a man or woman, Mr. Prince?"

Oh, God, no, he thought to himself. "A woman. What happened? Is she . . ." He couldn't say "dead." "Is she okay?"

"She was taken to the hospital. I haven't been able to confirm the injuries. Do you have a reaction?"

"Oh, Lord, I didn't know."

"May I quote you?"

"I've got to go. Goodbye." He slammed the phone down and called the front desk, but no one had been on duty when the attack happened. No one knew what hospital she'd been taken to or the extent of her injuries, but everyone knew that Persy had been attacked on her way home from the casino, as she walked through the bushes in the dark.

He ran his hand through his hair. Where was she? How was she? *Oh, Persy! Not you!*

He turned and ran from his office, took the steps three at a time, and was out of the building. He ran across the parking lot, past the police lines that showed where the robbery had taken place. Hurdling the low fence, he ran down the street toward Persy's house faster than he could ever remember moving. Impatient, he knocked on the door three times, then knocked again.

"Just a minute, give me a chance to get there." Susan opened the door.

"How's Persy? What happened?" he demanded. He saw Frank behind his mother. "How is she?" Frank turned away from him.

"She has a dislocated shoulder. She hurts all over but she's lucky there's nothing serious. No internal injuries," Susan answered in a flat voice. "No thanks to you, of course."

"Where is she?"

"She's here, on the sofa."

"Why isn't she in the hospital?"

"They wanted to keep her at least twenty-four hours but, if you don't know why she didn't stay, you don't know Persy very well. She said that one of the reasons there's a health care crisis in this country is because people who don't need to be in the hospital are kept there and too many tests are run. She got a prescription and we brought her home."

"Can I see her?"

"Why do you want to see her, man?" Frank said. "My mom may be afraid to tell you what she thinks because she owes her job to you, but we're all angry. If you'd listened to us when we tried to tell you, this wouldn't have happened. And to Persy! After my mom, she's the best person I know."

"If it's any consolation to you, I won't forgive myself." Jordan looked Frank in the eye. "I'd decided to do the work but hadn't gotten it contracted out yet." He asked Susan again, "Can I see her?"

"Let him in." Persy's voice, soft and with a tiny quaver, came from the sofa.

"How are you doing?" Jordan shouldered past Susan and kneeled down next to the sofa.

"Okay. A little woozy. They gave me a pain shot."

He stood. "What happened?"

"I was coming back from work and this guy tried to take my purse. I shouted and Frank came but not before the thief took my purse."

"She fought so hard, the guy dislocated her shoulder when he pulled on the purse," Susan said.

"Why didn't you give it to him? Why did you fight?" Jordan was so relieved she was okay, he felt like crying.

"Sometimes when I'm angry, I do stupid things."

He nodded. "May I sit down? Will it hurt if I sit next to you?" He noticed her nails were broken and her fingers and the backs of her hands were covered with scratches. "You must have fought hard." He turned to Frank, who was standing guard at the foot of the sofa.

"How'd you get there so fast, Frank?"

The young man shrugged. "I know Persy's shifts and I wait on the porch until she's home. When I heard her screams, I shouted for my brothers and the other guys in the neighborhood. We have sort of a patrol. But, by the time I got there, the guy had run and Persy was hurt."

"May I use the phone?" Jordan asked.

"Sure," Persy said.

Jordan stood, picked up the phone, and called the day manager at the hotel. "Tom, I want you to get maintenance to work *now* on cutting out all the bushes where the accident happened. They can't cross police lines, of course. You call Terminal Electric and get them out here today to start putting up lights . . . I don't care how much it costs. I want it started NOW!" Then he whispered into the phone, "Go to the florists in the lobby and bring every flower you can find to 106 La Paloma. Charge it to my account."

He hung up and turned to Frank. "Thanks for watching out for her, Frank. You have full tuition and everything else to whatever school you want to go to. It's the only way I can think of to thank you. And any of your brothers or patrol members, too. Now, if you'll excuse me, I'm going to sit with Persy." He carefully sat next to her and took her hand. "I'm sorry, Persy. I really had started the paperwork on the changes, but I didn't take action soon enough. I feel really guilty."

"Guilt's good. Guilt brings change."

"Can you ever forgive me for being so stubborn?"

"Give me a while. I may think of some other changes I want made." She paused. "Jordan," she whispered. "I was really scared."

"It was a frightening situation, Persy. That's normal."

"Not for me." She settled her head onto his shoulder. "I'm so glad you're here." Her eyes closed and she fell asleep, her breath coming in soft snores that blew warm on his cheek.

"She's alive," Jordan repeated. He smiled a little, " 'And the Grinch's heart grew ten sizes that day.' "

* * *

I'm hungry and I need to go to the bathroom, Persy thought when she awakened. Unsteadily, she sat up and looked around. Vases of roses covered the dresser, potted plants were scattered around the floor, and bouquets of various kinds and colors of flowers were positioned on every other open space.

"Where did these come from?" she asked groggily. "Did someone's garden explode?"

"I know you like flowers." She turned to see Jordan sitting on the floor next to her bed. "There are a few more in the rest of the house."

"Oh, how sweet." She smiled at him, then felt her face with her hands and looked in dismay at her ratty flannel gown. "What are you doing here? I look terrible."

He decided not to respond to her final statement. "I wanted to visit you, to tell you how sorry I am this happened."

She nodded. "I'm hungry," she said.

"What do you want to eat? Think of anything. I'll get it for you."

"I've been dreaming about the broccoli and cheese soup they serve in the Crown Room. Can you get me some of that?"

"In no time at all. Stay here. I'll get female help for you." Jordan stood and stretched, then stuck his head out the door to address Susan. "Help her to the restroom."

After Susan took over, Jordan moved a vase of orange tulips to get to the phone. He called the hotel kitchen and ordered a quart of soup to be brought to Persy's house, then entered the kitchen to make a sandwich. The amount of food on the counter and in the refrigerator astounded him: buckets of chicken, a hot brisket, salads, vegetable casseroles, cakes, and pies.

"Where'd all this food come from?" he asked Frank, who seemed to be on continual watch.

"Everyone in El Valle loves Persy. We knew she'd need food since she can't work for a while, so we started bringing it. My mom took some home to freeze. We had to make a schedule of who was going to stay with Persy," Frank added. "Otherwise, there would've been ten people here around the clock. Of course, you're pretty much taking care of all of it."

"I'm sorry. I didn't mean to step on toes. It's just that—" He didn't know how to finish his thought.

"You feel guilty."

"It's not only that, but I do feel guilty."

"You should. But I guess you know that. You go ahead and sit with her. You're going to have to go back to work one of these days, but we'll still be here. Neighbors take care of each other in El Valle."

A woman he didn't know cut him a piece of chocolate cake and handed it to him. "How that poor girl's going to work, I don't know. She can't deal or be a waitress with one arm."

"Worker's compensation. If that doesn't work, the hotel will pay her. She can sue us. Don't worry, she'll have enough to live on until she's okay."

"Well, I'm mighty glad to hear that. We can cook up a storm and give each other love and support but we're short on cash. Now, you go back and take care of her."

Jordan spent the night in the chair next to Persy's bed. When he awoke, he was so stiff he didn't know if he could stand. He turned to find Persy already awake and looking at him. "How are you this morning?" he asked.

"Much better. I'm hungry." As she struggled to get out of bed, with Jordan's help, she asked, "Do I look as bad as I feel?"

"You've got a big bruise on your cheek. Did the guy hit you?"

"I don't remember. Everything happened so fast. But it looks like it, doesn't it?"

He leaned over to kiss her, then pulled back.

"What's the matter?"

"I don't want to hurt you."

"Just kiss me."

He did.

Chapter Eight

"How much recycled paper do you use in your hotel chain?" Persy was propped up on pillows on the sofa, reading the newspaper.

"None." Jordan didn't even pause as he read some of the mail Martha had brought to Persy's house earlier that day.

"Why not?"

"Because recycled paper costs more than the type that isn't."

"So?" Persy put the paper down and glared at Jordan. "That's because federal law favors paper companies that cut down trees and don't use recycled materials. Don't you care about the environment?"

"That's the way it's set up." Jordan looked up. "I'm running a business. I have to keep costs down to keep profits up."

"But in twenty years, the landfills—"

"If I'm lucky, I won't be running the business in

twenty years and I know I won't be worried about landfills, ever."

"Are you using recycled motor oil in the limos and vans?"

"No. You can't do that." Jordan returned to the letter he was perusing.

"Oh, yes you can! Oil doesn't wear out. It only gets dirty. Did you know Germany re-refines eighty-five percent of its used oil?"

"Hmmm."

"Landfills receive eleven million tons of paper a year."

"Fascinating." He continued to read the letter.

"There are more important things in life than profit margins."

"Spoken like someone who doesn't run a business." He glanced up. "Tell that to your people in El Valle if they lose a job because our profits are down."

"Oh, you're never going to change!" Persy buried her head in the newspaper.

Jordan stood, walked to the sofa, and took the newspaper from her. "I thought there were some ways in which you didn't want me to change." He sat next to her and placed kisses on the area of her face that wasn't bruised.

"If I could use both arms, I'd pull you down and get a real kiss."

"Will this do?" Jordan gently massaged her mouth with his lips. "Persy, even with your injuries and bruises, you pack more punch than any woman I've ever known."

"But I look so terrible. How can you want to kiss a woman who looks like this?"

"I close my eyes."

She shook her head.

"Persy, you do look better, a lot less like a prune." He dodged a pillow Persy swung at hit him. "The bruise is turning yellow. Looks more like you have jaundice now. Do you want a mirror?"

"I don't think I'm ready for that yet. I looked at myself Sunday morning and vowed I wouldn't look again for a week."

"How do you feel?"

"A little sore."

"If you'd take a pain pill occasionally . . ."

"I would if I needed to, but I can handle it. I don't want to take any medication."

"You are the most stubborn woman."

"And you're Mr. Flexible?"

"I wasn't talking about me." He looked at his watch. "I've got to go back to the office for about an hour. I'll be back to tutor Frank."

"I can . . ."

"I want to. I owe him that and more."

"He told me about the tuition. That was nice."

"Kid has a big mouth." Jordan slipped his shoes on and picked up the mail. "I won't be able to come over tomorrow at all. I've got to go to Ventura for a meeting. I'll have to leave really early in the morning and won't be back until Thursday morning. I'm sorry."

"I understand. I'll miss you, but it's been wonderful having you here all this time. You're a wonderful nurse."

"That wasn't what I was hoping you'd think."

"What were you hoping?"

"I don't know, really. I'm pretty sure nurse wasn't it. Something a little less wholesome." He opened the door and shouted back into the house. "Goodbye, Agatha."

"Goodbye," she called from her bedroom.

What had he hoped? Jordan wondered as he headed back toward the hotel. He paused for a moment, pleased to see that the area was cleared of bushes and that lights covered the area between El Valle and the hotel. Finally, he returned to his previous thought: what had he hoped she'd think of him if he stayed at the house and took care of her?

Was he hoping she'd see that he was truly a prince of a man and fall in love with him? Why would he want her to fall in love with him? He wasn't in love with her. A prince didn't fall in love with a commoner except in the movies.

If he wasn't in love with her, why had he spent three days in the house, leaving only to shower and pick up clothes?

Guilt? Of course, there was that, but guilt wasn't the complete answer. She attracted him, he knew. He needed to play out that attraction but he most certainly wasn't in love with her. Not Jordan Prince. Jordan Prince had never lost his heart to anyone. It gave him great pleasure to take care of her now.

"So you don't know how it feels to fall in love?" he could hear his mother saying. "Maybe it means you sit with her when she's hurt and hold her when she's frightened and spend all day in an uncomfortable chair to be with her and cover her home with flowers because you know she likes them."

"No," he answered out loud, to convince himself. "I don't even know her, really. We don't talk, we argue. We have nothing in common except that attraction. I'll stick around until that goes away."

But he feared he was fooling himself.

He missed her, really missed her. Being with her was like warming his face in the sun, like holding his hands up to a blazing fire. Being away was cold and lonely. When he wasn't with her . . . He made himself stop the thought, afraid where it might lead.

He looked out the plane's window on the way to Ventura. To the east, he could see the sunrise and wished he were in El Valle watching it with her. He wanted to talk to her. He looked at the telephone on the back of the seat in front of him. No, that was stupid. He didn't need to talk to her. He'd read his business magazine.

Jordan's resolution held for fifteen more minutes. When he realized he hadn't read a paragraph of the article, he gave up, took out his credit card and slid it through the phone. After he dialed her number, he counted the rings.

"Hello?" Agatha answered.

"Hi, Agatha. This is Jordan. Is Persy up?"

"No, but she'd kill me if I didn't call her, and I'm going to die soon enough. Hold on. I'll take her the phone."

"Hi," a sleepy voice answered. "Where are you?"

"On the plane. I saw the phone and wanted to call you."

"Is that cost-effective?" Persy teased.

"No, but it's not as expensive as thinking of you

during the entire meeting and wishing I had called you earlier."

"Would you do that? Think of me?"

"I'm afraid so."

"How nice."

"But not good business. I'll call you tonight."

"Are you sure I'll be here? I might be out with some other millionaire."

"There's not a man in the world who'd want to be seen in public with your face that color." He paused for a moment, uncertain. "Will you be home?"

"Oh, all right. I'll be here."

By Saturday, Persy could cover most of the discoloration with makeup. She'd taken a bath but couldn't lift her arm to shampoo her hair.

"Would you help me wash my hair?" Persy asked.

"Me?" Jordan dropped the newspaper he'd been reading into his lap.

"Do you see anyone else here?" She looked around the room.

"I've noticed Agatha discreetly slips away when I come but I bet we could find her in the bedroom."

"She's watching her favorite Saturday programs. Do not disturb."

"You could call Susan."

"Sammy and Paul have baseball games this morning."

"Okay, what do I need to do?"

"You'll need to come to the sink first. Now, I'm going to turn the water on and lean over to wet my hair . . . Okay, it's wet enough. Rub the shampoo in. Come on. I know you've washed your hair before and it's the same. Or do you have a man who washes your hair?"

"Of course not. I wash my own hair."

"Well, it's exactly the same."

"I don't think so. I've never done this for a woman. It seems very intimate."

"Well, it's not. I have all my clothes on."

"Maybe I'd feel more comfortable if you didn't have all your clothes on. Perhaps if you'd take something off, I'd enjoy this more."

"Shut up and wash!"

"Yes, ma'am."

Actually, Persy thought, it was more than just intimate. She could feel Jordan's warmth next to her, so close, while his hands rubbed intricate patterns on her head.

"Now what?"

"Turn on the spray and rinse it off."

"Okay. Is the temperature right?"

"Stop, stop! You're drowning me! You're supposed to rinse the soap off my hair, not spray the water up my nose!"

"Complain, complain, complain. I'm sure that helped you heal. Now what?"

"The rinse. It's in the yellow bottle."

When that was finished, he handed her a towel and she rubbed her hair dry.

"Do you roll it?" Jordan watched Persy shake her head before she roughed up the curls with her left hand.

"No, it dries like that."

"In those cute little curls?"

"You like my curls?"

"I think they're marvelous. Funny curls, funny eyes."

"Hey, Persy." Sammy, Susan's youngest son, ran into the house, the screen door slamming shut behind him. "Are you going to the game?"

"I wouldn't miss it for the world," Persy said. "This is for first place in your division, isn't it?"

"Yeah, and it's really important."

"I'll be there to cheer for you. Before she left for Paul's game, your mom asked me to fix you a sandwich. It's on the kitchen table."

"Are you sure you're up for this?" Jordan asked with concern after Sammy left. "With all your bruises, how long are you going to be comfortable on the bleachers."

"None of the bruises are where I sit."

"Persy." He held her shoulders gently and looked into her eyes. "You know what I mean. It hasn't even been a week since you were hurt. How long are you going to be able to sit in the bleachers?"

"I don't know. But I always go to Sammy's games."

"I'll go and root for him. Why don't you stay here and rest? He'll understand."

"But he expects me to be there." She put her hand uncertainly on her bruises.

"Persy, stay here. I'll go."

"You will?" She looked into his eyes. "How very nice of you. Thank you."

When Sammy came back in the room, still chewing his sandwich, Persy said, "You know, I'm still a little sore, Sammy. Would it be okay if Mr. Prince went to the game with you?"

"Mr. Prince? Thank you, sir. That's really great. I'd really like that."

That's how he ended up on a Saturday afternoon, sitting in the slight shade of two pitiful mesquite trees with all the other mothers and fathers, watching a kid he'd known for a few weeks play baseball. Was he enjoying it? Well, yes. Actually, unexpectedly, he was.

"Let's you and me do some throwing some afternoon," Jordan suggested after Sammy's team had triumphed.

"Thank you, sir." Sammy sucked on the soda Jordan had bought him. "Persy taught me to hit and field."

"Persy taught you that?"

"Yeah. Mom said she was a real good athlete when she was young."

Jordan grinned. Another fascinating item about Persy's past to tuck away.

That evening, Jordan and Persy sat on the porch swing and watched the neighbors walk up and down visiting while others went to and returned from work. Agatha sat inside watching a horror show on television. He could hear an occasional scream from the living room.

"Sammy was telling me that you were a great athlete when you were younger." Jordan put his arm around Persy and held her as close as her bruises allowed.

"When I was younger! I didn't realize I was over the hill yet."

"What did you play?"

"Almost everything. I had an older brother and a neighborhood full of guys who taught me."

"Were you any good?"

"Yeah, pretty good."

"Did you play sports in high school?"

"Yes."

"You know, in a conversation, you're supposed to help a little. This isn't supposed to be an interrogation."

"I feel uncomfortable talking about the past. It feels like bragging about a person I'm not anymore." She grimaced and sighed. "Okay. Yes, I played sports in high school and college."

"In college, too? What sports? Did you receive a scholarship?"

"I was best in basketball. Had twenty scholarship offers."

"Twenty? My gosh, you must have been terrific. All in basketball?"

"No, a couple were in softball and skiing."

"Skiing?"

"But I don't like cold weather. I chose Stanford because of the education I'd receive and I could still play sports."

"I bet you were a feisty little point guard with a great outside shot."

"How did you know?"

"Well, you're little and feisty and always telling everyone what to do. The outside shot was a guess." As the traffic on the street became lighter, Jordan pulled Persy closer and began kissing her neck. "I wish we could have some private time. Why don't you come to my suite in the hotel?"

"Absolutely not, Mr. Prince." Persy pulled away from him.

"What? Why not?"

"Mr. Prince, surely you know that everyone on the staff knows you take your fancy ladies there."

"My fancy ladies? What are you talking about? You know that?"

"Everyone knows that."

"Oh. Now I'm really embarrassed. I seem to have led a past I wish you didn't know so much about. But I'm trying to reform."

"By asking me to go to your suite? I think you need to try harder."

"Please, please, please go to my suite with me."

"No!" She laughed. "I meant you need to try harder to reform. You know, as much as I'd like privacy with you, I'm not sure you'd enjoy me very much."

"Let me see."

"No, I should have said I wouldn't enjoy it. I still have aches in funny places and if I move, it hurts."

"Okay, I'll drop it, reluctantly, but only until you're feeling better."

"I brought chips and salsa. Can't watch a baseball game without chips and salsa." Jordan put his plastic bags in the kitchen and took a soda out of the cooler.

"Bring me a root beer, would you, please?" Persy adjusted the color on the ancient set as Jordan settled on the couch and pulled her down next to him.

"Okay, you guys can have the sofa but where are the rest of us going to sit?" Frank entered with his brothers.

"Hey, I don't want to watch them fooling around on the sofa all night long. Can't you guys go some-place private?" Frank's brother Julio said.

"I thought we were." Jordan sat up and Barbarella jumped in his lap. "I forget this house is the community center. Come on in, guys. Are you planning to watch the baseball game with us? There's food in the kitchen."

When Jordan finished his soda, he moved the cat, stood, and started to toss the can in the wastebasket.

"No, no!" shouted Persy. "Wash it out and leave it in the sink."

"Oh, of course, you recycle."

"Of course!"

"Saving the universe one can at a time."

"Did you know that Americans throw enough aluminum away every three months to rebuild our entire commercial air fleet?" Frank asked.

"I don't know if I want to fly in a plane made out of old root beer cans." Jordan tossed it into the trash.

"Recycling only one aluminum can saves enough energy to run this television for the entire game," Julio added.

"I should have realized you've all been indoctrinated. Okay, okay, I'll take care of it." He picked up the can, washed it out, and opened the cupboard under the sink. "Hey, Persy, I can't find the sack for the can. This whole thing is filled with paper bags. Why do you have so many?"

"I reuse them," Persy came into the kitchen. "When I go to the grocery store, I always ask for paper sacks so I can save them and take them with me the next time I go to the store."

"If you do that, why are there so many bags under the counter?"

"Because I always forget to take them back. But I will! Someday!"

Jordan was suddenly very quiet and thoughtful. "I had an idea, Persy. Let me think for a minute." He sat down at the kitchen table. "What would you think . . ." he began slowly. "I want to hire you, at least part-time, to be in charge of the hotel's recycling effort."

"The hotel doesn't have a recycling effort."

"No, not until now. I want you to start it. I want you to indoctrinate—no, let me say educate—everyone the way you have here in the neighborhood. If you can make me wash out and save a can, you've really accomplished something. I want you to see what we need to be recycling, what we can cut down on. Appeal to the guests to conserve energy. Make signs. Send out memos. Teach classes."

"I can't do that. Have you forgotten? I have a bad shoulder."

"This is an executive position. You'll use Martha as your secretary and we'll have any signs you need made and you get to order people around. What do you think?"

"Well, I'm very good at that, but why do you want to do this? Is this charity because I can't work? Are you still feeling guilty?"

"Yes, I'm still feeling guilty but this isn't charity. I didn't realize how much difference recycling makes until Frank and Julio gave me those examples. That's amazing. But, additionally, it'll be great PR. I don't think there's a hotel chain in America that's big on recycling—other than that not washing the sheets stuff. It's a great story! This could be good for business as well as for the environment. We'll start a pilot project here and, if it works, we'll phase it in all over the United States, in forty-seven hotels. What do you say?"

"I think it's really exciting. Yes, I'd love to do it. When do I start?"

"How 'bout Monday of next week. Do you feel strong enough? You can start off part-time."

"Part-time? I'm ready for full-time! Can't I start tomorrow?"

Persy spent the first few days surveying the hotel, discovering areas of waste.

"The laundry wraps each sheet individually. We don't need that. That's extra packaging. They also buy detergent and fabric softener in plastic jugs instead of in the concentrated form that saves on plastic. What authority do I have?" Persy asked Jordan. She was meeting with him in his office a few days later.

"Probably a good idea to run it by me until you have a good feel for who you need to talk to in which departments. I think the laundry suggestions are fine. Go ahead."

"I also want to print up some little signs to put next to the thermostats in the guest rooms." She handed Jordan her copy:

If everyone in the USA lowered the settings of their air conditioners by 6 degrees, we'd save the energy equivalent of 500,000 barrels of oil a day!

Please remember, when you leave your room:
- Don't leave your air conditioning on COLD.
- Turn off the lights and television.

"Looks good to me."

"In the laundry, we're using hot water."

"I think we have to keep it at a certain setting due to health regulations but check with Sarah in the laundry to be sure."

"I'd like to have a contest to award staff who come up with good green suggestions. Maybe twenty dollars for a weekly winner, and a free dinner for two in the roof garden for a monthly winner. What do you think?"

"How much is this going to cost me?"

"Not that much. It's going to save you much more than that in the long run. Besides, as you pointed out, it's good public relations. Also good for employee morale."

"Okay. Get going."

"Thanks. I'm really having a wonderful time." Persy smiled at him and hurried from the room.

"I thought," Jordan said to the closed door, "I'd at least get an occasional kiss out of this." He hit the button on the intercom. "Martha, can you come in, please."

"Sorry, Mr. Prince, I can't. Persy left me some stuff she needs me to type: a memo to the staff for suggestions that she says you've approved and some things you wanted to go to PR."

Jordan put his head down on his desk. "I've even lost my secretary!" he groaned.

From then on, Jordan got into the end of conversations on shower head conversions, reuse of office materials like file folders, and solar power. "A dream."

Persy calmed him down about the idea of solar panels. "Maybe years in the future."

Signs went up in the guest bathrooms stating that showers took half as much hot water as baths and saved energy. A sign over the soda machines asked for cans to be recycled either by bringing them back to the bins in the snack areas or by washing them out in the room for the maid to pick up the next morning.

Green bins sprouted in the offices for used paper, which Persy made into scratch pads. Styrofoam cups were seen no more in the employee lounge. Each worker had to bring a pottery mug from home.

"I never figured you for a yellow roses type," one of the maintenance men teased another as they took a coffee break.

"Aw, my wife couldn't find another one. I gotta tell ya, I think the coffee tastes better in this cup."

Persy watched the two men from the kitchen where she was putting away the dry dishes. Jordan was helping Frank with his trig.

"Okay, let me look at this problem. What do you think you need to do to work it?"

"Well," Frank began. "I need to solve the problem to show . . ."

Jordan was a good teacher, not giving the answer but helping Frank to figure it out himself. Frank seemed to enjoy working with him. How strange: the scion of one of the richest families in America tutoring the son of migrant farm workers who'd settled in El Valle to improve his education.

Barbarella had come from Agatha's bedroom the

moment Jordan entered the door. The little cat had curled up on his right foot, purring happily.

"Yeah, hey, I can see that!" Frank turned toward Persy with enthusiasm after he solved the problem. "This guy's really great. I think you finally found a good one, Persy." Frank turned back toward Jordan. "You can't believe the losers she dates—when she can find a date."

"Frank, that's enough!" Persy warned. "Stick to the books!"

"Mr. Prince, the last guy, well, you wouldn't believe him."

"Frank!"

"That's okay, Frank," Jordan interrupted. "You and I can get together sometime and talk about Persy's past romantic involvements. It sounds like a fascinating topic. But, for now, let's work on trig. And please call me Jordan."

"Do you guys want to take a break for ice cream?" Persy asked, hoping to change the subject. "How 'bout chocolate sundaes?"

"Sounds good to us," Frank and Jordan agreed.

After she prepared and served their sundaes, Persy watched the two men at the table, talking and eating their ice cream. She compared the Jordan she'd seen in his tux, so sophisticated, to this relaxed man who was working with Frank and seeming to truly enjoy it. He even had a little bit of chocolate on his beautiful knit shirt and didn't seem to mind.

"Persy, do you dust your light bulbs?" Jordan studied the fixture in the middle of the ceiling

"Dust the light bulbs? Of course not."

"Did you know that you lose about ten percent of

the light when there is dust on the bulb? Tsk, tsk, tsk," Jordan scolded.

"Since when did you start spouting facts about conserving energy?" Persy laughed. "And, no, I haven't in the past and never will dust my light bulb."

"Wasting energy, my dear. Polluting the environment."

"Can't anyone watch television around here in silence?" Agatha opened the door of her room and shouted over the laughter.

Frank looked at the wall clock. "Nine o'clock. Time for me to go to home." He stood and picked up his books. "Thanks a lot for your help, Mr. Prince. You're a great teacher. I hope you can help me again."

After Frank left, Jordan turned to Persy. "Now that I have you alone, do you want to tell me about the disastrous romances in your past?" He took her hands and pulled her toward the sofa.

"No confessions." Persy laughed as she sat beside him. "Although I have to admit I haven't made the smartest choices—in the past, of course."

"Yes, your taste seems to have improved a great deal." Jordan leaned over and kissed her gently.

Persy's emotions were in turmoil. Until recently, she'd thought there was no future with Jordan, that this was another one of her disastrous relationships, but when he was so relaxed and at ease, so happy in her world, she began to wonder as he deepened the kiss.

"Not tonight. Perhaps another evening."

He leaned back and looked into her face, lifting an eyebrow in an implied question.

"It's just that sometimes I'm not sure exactly who

you are." She moved away reluctantly. "You've seemed so different since the . . . incident. Why? Where's the man you used to be?"

"I don't know. I walked into this house that night and saw you sitting there in that sling, and the world seemed to shift and settle into place. My priorities changed. I knew what was important. After that, it felt good to be here, comfortable. Strange, huh? I enjoy tutoring Frank and going to Sammy's games and having you around and being here—even Barbarella and Agatha with all her grumbling. I feel like a different person."

Persy smiled and tried to hide a yawn.

"I'd better go. You're exhausted. Walk me to the door?" Jordan stood up. "Kiss me goodnight? I've been so good tonight, don't you think I deserve a kiss?"

"Oh, you think you *deserve* a kiss?"

"Well, maybe not deserve, but I'd really like one."

"You're incorrigible, aren't you?" Persy put her arms around his neck and enjoyed the feel of his mouth on hers as heat zipped to her toes.

"Okay," he said when he reluctantly stepped away from her. "You go to bed, but I'll be back for more."

"I'm counting on that."

Everything seemed so perfect, so wonderful. It was about this time that something terrible happened in most of her relationships. Did he have a wife somewhere? Was she going to pull one of her sensational stunts to drive him away?

What was going to happen to mess this one up?

Chapter Nine

"Isn't it wonderful?" Persy twirled in front of the two-story brick fourplex a few weeks later. Her sling was off and the pain was gone, or so she insisted.

"Well, it looks very solid." Jordan pretended to examine the building but instead kept his eye on the joyful Persy. Her hair bounced with each step and her enormous smile forced his lips to curve up. She was so filled with delight that he couldn't help but feel wonderful. Her brilliant happiness dazzled him. He wanted to hold her and crush her to him, to share some of the glow that radiated from her. But, he didn't want to diminish that blaze. Instead, he watched her, feeling like the moon reflecting her fire. "Why are you so excited about this?"

It was early evening. Jordan and Persy had been strolling down La Paloma when Persy had suddenly tugged on his hand and led him to the apartments.

"It's my dream." Persy sat on the front step. "There are four apartments and a large basement. If I could buy it, I'd live in one of the apartments and put people who've lost their homes in the others." Unable to stay still, she stood and faced the building, pointing out where she'd live. Swirling around, she faced Jordan and threw her arms out to the side. "Can you see it? The basement could be used for community meetings and Boy and Girl Scout meetings, as a clothes and food closet, even more room for the literacy program. Over there," she said as she walked toward the small parking lot and large side yard, "we could have games for the children, build a day care someday, with a grant. The possibilities are endless!"

He sat on the step and pulled her down next to him. "Now, explain this again: who'd live in the other apartments?"

"People who have lived in their own homes or apartments before but lost them. They'd be a sort of transitional unit from being homeless to being able to afford housing again. I'd work with the shelters to find out who'd benefit from the service."

"How do you plan to finance this?"

Her expression lost its radiance. "That's what makes it a dream. I've applied for some grants but still haven't heard anything from some. Others have turned me down because the economy's so bad. But the place is for sale and it never hurts to dream. Doesn't it have exciting possibilities?"

"Have you seen the inside?"

"When it first went on sale, about three months ago. There's some work to be done, painting and cleaning, but it's in good condition other than that. Maybe," Persy bit her lip before she continued, "maybe a law office there for those who needed cheap legal advice. Or a clinic—"

"You know, you don't have to supply everything for the neighborhood. Others could get involved."

"I know. They would. I haven't shared this with anyone else yet. Only you."

Jordan felt ridiculously pleased that she'd told him before anyone else. "Have you talked to the State University Hospital? They've been putting clinics into poor areas. And the school system has literacy programs you might be able to tap into."

"Jordan." Persy looked at him with such delight on her face that he wished he could come up with a thousand more suggestions. "What wonderful ideas! I hadn't thought of that. Barb could check with the hospital. I wonder where we could find a place. Brownie knows every inch of this area. If anyone could, he could find an empty building for a clinic."

"The hotel owns a building over on Margarita Street that no one's using. Maybe we could work out a deal."

"Would you do that?" Persy looked into his face with such brilliance he was almost dizzy. "Why would you do that?"

"I'm sure," Jordan attempted to assume a business-like demeanor, "that a medical clinic in the area would improve the health of our employees and their families, meaning fewer sick days and more productivity."

"That will sound good for the board." Persy grinned up at him. "But, I know why you're suggesting that."

"Why is that?"

"Because you're really a wonderful, loving, caring person, although you try not to show it." She pulled his head down and kissed him.

"No, I'm not," he confessed when, after the kiss, he put his arm around Persy and pulled her close. "At least, I wasn't before I met you. You've changed me, Persy. You've made me grow and change. I wasn't sure that I liked the new me but I discover I do. Thank you." He gave her a hug. "But before the neighbors begin to talk about us for kissing in the middle of the street . . ."

"Oh, the neighbors already talk about us. Didn't you know that?"

He stood and took her hand and the two began to walk back to the house. "I guessed as much. What do they say?"

"That Jordie Prince . . ."

"Jordie? They call me Jordie?"

"It's meant as a compliment. Now, let me finish. They say that Jordie Prince is a fine man, a much better person than that L. Jordan Prince who used to work at the hotel." They entered Persy's house.

"I'm afraid, Persy, that you've turned me into a human being and I like it. What's your work schedule tomorrow?"

"I'm speaking at a businessmen's luncheon tomorrow on the recycling program. The program chair read the newspaper article and thought it sounded interesting so he gave me a call. Your PR department is good at getting the word out."

"That's what they're paid to do. And this weekend?"

"Did you have something planned?"

"Speaking of the weekend," Agatha came to the door. "My friend Burt has invited me to Sunday dinner. Can you get me to his retirement center for Sunday dinner? Is there a bus?"

"Don't even consider a bus, Agatha," Jordan sat on the swing. "I'll drive you there. Is it noon dinner?"

"Of course, young man. Do you think this is one of your swanky dining rooms with dinner at eight o'clock with music and candles? No sir." She turned back toward the house. "We'll need to leave by eleven."

"Won't that get us there a little early?" Jordan asked.

"Burt's invited me to see his apartment," Agatha confessed as she ran back into the house.

"Well, well," Jordan laughed. "I think if we could have seen her face, we could have seen her blushing."

"I guess this is serious if Agatha's been invited to see his room." Persy said. "This will be a busy weekend, with the neighborhood picnic Saturday and Agatha's trip Sunday. I can't wait to meet the man who can make Agatha blush."

Her concentration is amazing, Jordan thought as he watched Persy. She'd been the first chosen for the team and he could see why. As shortstop, she gobbled up every ball that came near her, throwing the runners out with strong throws. He'd purposely hit a ball to her, which she fielded and flipped to first with little effort.

"She's good, isn't she?" Jordan turned to Susan. They sat on the bench in the shade, awaiting their turns at bat.

"Yeah, she's good at everything she tries. Persy wouldn't allow herself to fail at anything."

"You sound a little critical."

"You mean, why is her best friend trashing her? I'm not. I love her dearly, but those who know her well know that Persy looks like a pansy but she's a barracuda at heart. You had the run-in with her about our right-of-way. We didn't ask Persy to handle that only because she's a lawyer. We knew that once she got started, she wouldn't give up."

"I didn't see anything out of the ordinary."

"That's because you didn't hold out very long. Persy's the kind who would chain herself to the bushes and refuse to eat until you gave in."

They paused for awhile, watching a Persy field a slow ball toward second. Never taking her eye off the ball, she ran toward it, picked it up, and with a spinning move threw it toward second. Jordan picked up his mitt and went to play third base.

Persy was the lead-off batter. He saw her look at him, standing about five feet off the base. She took a ball before she dug in behind the plate. The pitch came and she guided it down the line, between him and the bag. It went all the way to the fence while she sprinted around the bases, stopping at third when the ball came back to the infield.

"Good hit."

"Thanks."

"Yeah, she is a barracuda," Jordan said to Susan as they sat on the bench the next inning. "But everyone in the neighborhood and at the hotel thinks she's great. Why would they, if she's such a hard-nose?"

"Because we know she loves us. When she wants to do something in the neighborhood, it's for our own good."

Three ground balls were hit to Persy, so three play-ers were out. "Guess we're back in the field."

"Of course," said Susan after they'd both batted and scored, "I can understand why she's like this. Her mother is a real Southern belle, a lady who expected her daughter to be a lady. Persy had all she could take of that and rebelled."

"But she was a good athlete. How could a belle want her daughter to be an athlete?"

"Because Persy's ability made her mother look good." Susan shifted on the bench. "I feel as if I've really been gossiping about Persy and I didn't mean it that way. It's just that Persy frightens men off. I was hoping that wouldn't happen with you if maybe I could explain her a little, warn you."

"Most of what you said, I knew. Don't worry. She's not going to frighten me off."

"But to understand her, you've got to know that Persy's family was a lot like yours and she hated that life. Really hated it."

After the game was over, Jordan congratulated Persy on her team's victory. "Good game, tiger."

"Thanks." She lifted her eyebrow. "Tiger?"

"Watching you play, I discovered a new dimension to your personality."

"You of all people know most of it, how hardheaded I am." She studied his face for a moment and sighed. "I saw you and Susan talking the whole time. I sup-pose she told you all about my past." She made a face. "Well, I don't mind. I know Susan was trying to help me. She worries and she thinks you're a good influence." She picked up the sports equipment and put it in the bag. "I'm starving. Let's go get some food."

The rest of the afternoon was spent eating and playing volleyball. Jordan was amazed that the neighbors (most of them were his employees) were able to treat him not as a boss but as Persy's boyfriend.

"Explain something to me," Jordan asked as they walked back to Persy's house after the picnic. "Susan said your mother, the perfect Southern belle, wanted you to be an athlete. But I don't understand. Wouldn't she want you to be a simpering beauty?"

"No, she sort of lived through our accomplishments. But there was one rule I had to follow: never beat a boy at sports."

Jordan stopped under a street light and looked at Persy. "You're kidding me. I thought that kind of thinking went out fifty years ago."

"Not for a Southern belle. I'll never forget when she first told me. It was really a little amusing because I'd always thought that boys and girls should be treated equally."

"Silly you."

"Right. Silly me. I was at a swimming party in seventh grade and challenged a boy to a race. I beat him, easily. When I told Mother, she laughed and drawled, 'Darlin', no, no, no! You must never beat a boy or a man. They won't like being beaten by a girl.' "

"Well, she's right about that. We don't like it, but we're trying to do better." He smiled at her. "I don't think you learned your mother's lesson very well."

"Oh, but I did. Until college, I was very careful never to beat a boy in anything. I was a good athlete, in women's sports. I made good grades but never compared my grades to the grades of boys."

"And then?"

Persy smiled up at him. "And then I decided to make up for the wasted years. Now I try to beat men in whatever game they're playing."

"Turn right up here, at the light." Agatha pointed. She sat in the back seat, giving frequent directions to Jordan although she'd never been to the center before. They'd loaded up and taken off just after the early church service, with Agatha nagging them the entire morning.

"Thanks, but I think I'll go a way I know." Jordan passed the corner.

"Hmmph. You men think you know everything." Agatha sat back.

"It's okay. I know where El Torre is." Jordan maneuvered the Mercedes through traffic and onto the highway. "We'll be there by eleven-thirty."

"Your car is beautiful." Persy rubbed the leather upholstery. "What I like best is how smooth the ride is. It's hard to believe we're in a car at all."

"Be careful, Miss Marsh. You might get taken in by the luxuries wealth can supply."

"Never, Mr. Prince. I know what is truly precious in life."

"Where does it say you can't enjoy something expensive that you earned, something that gives you pleasure?"

"I don't know where it says that. I know that my philosophy tells me that if it's expensive, someone else could use the money to feed their children or get health care."

"Oh, Persy, stuff it for today," Agatha interrupted. "Sit back and enjoy and don't act so high and mighty and exceedingly good."

Jordan picked up Persy's hand from the seat and kissed it. "Listen and learn from Agatha. Relax and enjoy for today."

"Okay." Persy leaned back and began to play with the power window. "I can see that I'm outnumbered and outvoted so I'll pretend I'm one of the idle rich."

"Idle rich?" Jordan bellowed. "When have you ever seen me idle?"

"Oh, that's it, that's it!" Agatha pointed to a low white stucco structure that covered the block. "Burt said to pull into parking lot A and enter there." She was out of the car almost before it stopped and into the building before Persy could even open her door.

"This really is serious," Persy said as Jordan opened the door for her. "I've never seen her move so fast."

"This is Burt." Agatha took the hand of the tall white-haired man who stood next to her in the lobby, beaming down at her. "Isn't he gorgeous?"

"Oh, Agatha, I'm an old man." Smiling Burt reached out to shake hands with Jordan and Persy. "Glad to meet both of you."

"We're going to look at Burt's apartment before lunch." She nodded at Persy and Jordan. "Be back around two-thirty."

When Persy and Jordan returned after eating lunch and strolling through the park, they discovered a blissful Agatha holding hands with an equally happy Burt.

"Brace yourselves," Agatha said. Persy and Jordan looked at each other and then back at Agatha.

"We're getting married," she finally said. "In three weeks. There's a chapel here at the center. We signed up for it today. After the wedding, we'll live in Burt's apartment until something larger comes up."

"Oh, Agatha, I'm so happy for you . . . both!" Persy gave the elderly woman a hug.

"You can have the entire house to yourself," Agatha said. "Except, of course, I'll leave you Barbarella for company."

"Barbarella? You don't want to leave Barbarella behind."

"Well, there are rules here. No animals. But now I'll have Burt to keep me company. You need Barbarella and she'd really miss Jordan. He's the only one she really cares for."

"I wish you both happiness." Jordan shook hands with Burt and turned to hug Agatha. "And thank you. I'm sure my lap would be very lonely without Barbarella there."

The drive back was filled with Agatha's happy planning. "You will stand up with me, won't you, Persy?"

"I'll be delighted to, Agatha."

"Of course, we'll need to find you a suitable dress. Honestly, you have the most absurd clothes for a woman your age. If you think you can wear jeans or that ridiculous floating dress you wore for you first date with him, you can't. This is a wedding."

"I'll find something, Agatha."

The house would be lonely and silent without Agatha. Persy would be able to sit on the sofa until midnight, if she wanted to, she and Jordan could watch television late, as they had tonight, kissing, but not worrying about keeping Agatha awake. And Agatha was a good listener. Persy'd miss that, as well as her cooking and care.

Jordan had reminded her when he left that soon they'd have the house to themselves. It was a frightening thought. Persy wondered if she were ready to move to a different, deeper level in her relationship with Jordan. She was scared, terrified that she'd return to the woman she'd been before, the one who'd been so wrapped up in the luxuries Jordan could offer that she couldn't see the important things in life. The problem was that she genuinely cared for Jordan, as well as feeling so attracted to him. If she let the all these things take over, would she become a different Persy? Would she become Mary Persistence again?

Could she take a chance on loving Jordan? She feared she already did, despite her denial. Persy shivered. She was going to have to think all of this through before Agatha left, before the presence of the older woman couldn't protect her from the feelings Jordan aroused. Three weeks—that wasn't nearly enough time to sort through her feelings.

"There a couple of things I want to talk to you about." Jordan fought Persy for the last pieces of popcorn as they watched television. "You're going to be famous."

"Move your hand! You're not letting me get any popcorn." She pushed her hand under his. "What do you mean, I'm going to be famous?"

"That local morning show. 'Good Day, Gulf City,'

wants us to tape a segment for their show in two weeks, Friday the twenty-fifth."

"What? Us? Why?"

"To talk about the recycling project."

"Really?"

"Yes. They've set us up for a ten-minute segment."

"Do we need to rehearse? What do we do?"

"We just talk, that's all, and I know you can do that for hours. The problem will be to contain it in a few minutes."

"Of course I can."

"The second thing: the hotel chain is having their big corporate meeting here, in less than two weeks. I'd really like you to go to the party on Tuesday evening with me." Jordan put down the popcorn bowl and watched her.

"You mean, a really formal type of party?"

"Yes."

"Like long dresses and tuxes?"

"Yes."

Persy considered this. "Why do you want me to go with you?"

"Because, idiot, I enjoy being with you. Haven't I made that obvious? Also, I need you to talk up the recycling program."

"How long have you known about this?"

"A month or two."

"Why didn't you ask me sooner?"

"Because I knew you wouldn't be able to give me a simple 'yes.' I knew we'd go through all this questioning and wondering and discussion and vacillation. Finally I decided I didn't care how much of a hassle you made me go through. I want to be with you. So I'm asking."

"Oh. You think you know me pretty well?"

"Fairly well. Would you prefer I asked someone else, perhaps Adrienne or Daphne?"

"No."

"So your answer is?"

"Well, then, yes."

"Yes, what."

"Yes, I'll go with you."

"You will? Great." He sighed and leaned back, scratching Barbarella's ears as she purred. "That was easier than I'd expected. I thought I was going to have to throw in your clinic building as an incentive."

"What do you mean?"

"I was going to tell you that the board will be meeting to discuss the clinic the day after the party. At the party, you can meet the board members and persuade them."

"You mean play politics?"

"That's the way things are done, Pers. You have to learn to schmooze if you want to get things for the community."

"I know, and it's so hard for me. It seems manipulative and dishonest."

"Here, let me teach you about schmoozing with the boss." Jordan carefully moved Barbarella to another chair but not before the cat stopped purring and bit him. He turned toward Persy and pulled her against him. "You know, when Agatha leaves—"

Persy cut off his words. "Be happy with what we have now," she said, nibbling on his lower lip while the heat he so easily aroused spread through her.

"Sweetheart, happy doesn't begin to describe it." Jordan captured her lips.

As Persy turned and leaned back against the arm of the aged sofa, pulling Jordan close, she became aware of three things. First, Jordan made her temperature rise to an alarming level. Second, the old sofa was screeching with every move they made. Third, the television in Agatha's room had suddenly become silent. Persy could imagine the older woman's ear glued to the door.

"No, Jordan. Not now. Not with Agatha listening," she whispered.

With a disappointed groan, Jordan pushed away from her. "Someday she'll be gone."

And the thought scared Persy to death.

"Persy, telephone. It's your mother," Agatha called from the living room a few days later. She handed the receiver to Persy before disappearing into the kitchen.

Persy felt the familiar drop of her stomach as she contemplated another chat with her mother. She took a deep breath and said, "Hello, Mom. How are you and Dad?"

"Hello, Mary Persistence. We're fine. Aren't you getting tired of that place? When are you going to come home?"

"I'm very happy here, Mother. Certainly that's important to you."

"Pooh! How you can be happy working with a bunch of . . . oh, I know better than to say more. You're so protective of those people. Your sister was here last week."

"How is Dilly?"

"Diligence is fine. Finishing her orthopedic residency at Vanderbilt. She's marrying a surgeon at Christmas."

"Oh? Does this surgeon have a name?"

"I don't know. I didn't ask."

"But he is professionally acceptable?" Persy asked sarcastically, knowing the inflection would completely escape her mother.

"Oh, dear, yes! And your brother will be a father in October, after he returns from his tour of Europe. The reviews of his playing have been wonderful. They say he is one of the finest concert pianists in the world."

"How fortunate Fort was able to work fatherhood into his schedule."

"Isn't it, Mary Persistence? Your father and I are going to Berlin to hear him play."

"That's exciting."

"Now, if only I could get you settled, dear. Why don't you find some nice rich man down there and get married so I can stop worrying about you."

"I can take care of myself, without a man. Mother, you can stop worrying about me."

"No, darling, until you come to your senses, I will continue to fret. I am, after all, your mother."

"If I'm happy, that should be enough for anyone's mother. I'm happy. Stop brooding!"

"No, darling, you really need someone to take care of you, to return you to the ambiance you grew up in. I'll continue to hope." In her characteristic manner, Persy's mother hung up the phone without saying goodbye or letting Persy know the conversation was over.

"Nice to talk to you, Mother," Persy said into the dead line. "Tell Dad hello."

"There are two apartments up and two down," the real estate agent said as he unlocked the door of the fourplex. "Let me show you the nicest and largest." He went up a flight of steps and unlocked another door. "This one has two bedrooms and a small extra room. It was a nursery but could be a study. Nice carpet."

Jordan entered. The living room was larger than he'd guessed. Through an arch he saw the kitchen and eating area. The tile in the kitchen was fairly new. "It needs paint."

"Yes, in some areas but it depends on what you plan to do with it. If you want to live here, this would have to be painted, but if you rent it, it's in good enough condition."

You don't know Persy, Jordan thought. She'd expect every apartment to be perfect for anyone living there. "The bedrooms are this way?" He peeked into a small bathroom as he went down the hall toward the larger bedroom. Jordan stopped and opened the door to a small room. "Is this the nursery?"

The agent stepped in and flipped the light switch. Instantly, the paintings on the wall came alive. An earlier tenant had painted a magical forest scene on the walls of the tiny room. Trees started at the floor and branched out on the ceiling. In the forest were deer and unicorns and a magical mixture of creatures: lions and lambs, kittens and puppies. In the center, a baby crawled through the enchanted scene. Sunlight and love filled the painting with so much joy that Jordan found himself smiling.

"Persy would love this," Jordan whispered. "It's wonderful." For a moment, he pictured himself here with Persy, the two of them placing their baby in a crib, a yellow crib with ruffles, he imagined, and smiling at each other. Only the first in a line of babies he and Persy would place carefully and lovingly in that yellow crib in the room surrounded with gentle animals.

"Do you want to see the rest?"

"No, this is enough. How much are they asking?"

The agent named a figure.

"If part of this will be used for a federal housing program, what kind of financing are we looking at?" Jordan took a pad and pen from his pocket.

"There are several types," the agent began. He outlined the possibilities. "I suggest you check with your banker."

"I'll take it," Jordan said. "Let's talk figures." He left the agent's office with a contract and the keys in his pocket and went back to look at the fourplex.

"Idiot," he said aloud as he looked at the building. "You thought you were buying this as a present for Persy, for her to start her dream. Now you know. You're in love with her and plan to live here with her. How do you feel about that?"

"Terrific," he answered himself, grinning. "Absolutely terrific."

"Have you found a dress to wear to my wedding yet?" Agatha asked.

"I got this box of my old clothes down from the

attic," Persy said, plucking a cobweb from her hair. "These are things I didn't think I'd ever wear again but couldn't bear to throw away. Let's see if there's anything." She opened the box, tossed her Stanford sweatshirt aside and dug deep in the box. "Do you have a color preference?"

"No, just anything pastel."

"How 'bout this?" Persy held up a jonquil cotton dress with a wide embroidered ruffle around the neck and skirt.

"Maybe. What else do you have in there?"

Persy tossed out a navy tailored dress before she picked up a long black dress that shimmered in the afternoon sun.

"What's that?" Agatha held the dress up. Barbarella playfully swatted at the sequins.

"That's my favorite formal from college." Persy looked at it speculatively. "Maybe that's what I should wear to Jordan's party. Do I still have the shoes and purse?" She rummaged through the box and found them. "What do you think?"

"I think that would knock him off his feet."

"I'd love to knock Mr. L. Jordan Prince off his feet! I wonder if it's possible."

Chapter Ten

It *was* possible. Persy smiled with delight at Jordan's expression when he saw her. His eyes widened and his mouth dropped open.

She'd studied herself before he arrived and felt incredibly gorgeous, although she had a moment of misgiving. Was she returning to her earlier need for approval? But she banished the thought. She wanted to look beautiful for Jordan if only for tonight.

Susan had rolled her hair in large curlers so it waved back from her face. "Very sophisticated" was the verdict. She wore makeup, a little eye shadow and mascara that made her eyes look even larger, lipstick, powder, and blush. Agatha had bought her a pair of textured black hose with flowers somehow embroidered up the ankles—incredibly seductive. The dress was wonderful on her. Although a few years had filled out Persy's figure a little, the shimmering black gown fit sleekly. High heels and long, dangling earrings completed the picture.

She then dabbed a little perfume behind her ears, on her wrists, and between her breasts. It was a sophisticated scent she'd bought on impulse that afternoon and it made her feel seductive.

"You are the most beautiful woman I've ever seen." Jordan said after a moment of silence and a few inarticulate sounds.

"Thank you," she said with a demure glance that she could feel turning into a leer inside as she appreciated the breadth of his shoulders. She longed to touch that place where his hair swirled on the back of his neck, that one little place that wasn't completely perfect. "You look wonderful in a tux, but I knew that." She turned toward Agatha. "Don't wait up."

"She may never be home," Jordan said, capturing her hand and holding it by his side as Persy leaned into his strength. "I brought transportation worthy of such beauty." He escorted her down the steps and out to the limo.

Persy looked in surprise at the crowd that surrounded the car. Everyone in the neighborhood was there.

"We all had to see how you looked!" shouted Sammy.

"Wow, wow, wow!" said Frank.

"My thoughts exactly," Jordan laughed as he held the door open and Persy slipped inside.

The lawn of the house—no, mansion, Persy substituted—was larger than a football field and covered with striped tents, the sides of which were rolled up to display the glittering crowd. The light of lanterns strung throughout the grounds reflected off the extravagant jewels worn by the women, the immaculate white shirts of the men, and the crystal goblets carried by the waiters. As she stood in the middle of the lawn, Persy revolved slowly, marveling at the color and splendor of the surroundings.

Wouldn't this place wow mother? The thought stunned her. "It's really beautiful," she turned toward Jordan. "Who lives here?"

"My mother, although it is the family home. I grew up here and will inherit but right now it's hers."

Jordan still held her hand in such a way that she had to cuddle against his side—not that he had to use any force. She seemed to lean toward him as if he were the center of her universe and she an orbiting star.

"Ah, the Prince's Palace."

"So it's been dubbed. To me, it's just home."

" 'Be it ever so humble . . .' "

"Come on." He pulled her along behind him. "I have some people I'd like you to tell about the clinic and the recycling program."

Jordan introduced Persy to many of the directors of the hotel chain, with whom she discussed the hotel's recycling program. All displayed polite interest. A few asked for more details and, handing Persy their cards— "Do they never leave home without them?" Persy asked later—requested she call them to discuss more details.

"Schmoozing, huh? That's what I was doing?" she asked Jordan.

"And very well, too." Jordan grinned.

"I had an excellent model." She looked up at him and smiled.

"Thank you. You're an exceptionally talented and quick student. Now you can relax and pay attention to me, only me." Jordan placed his hand on her back and guided Persy around the lawn, nodding at friends.

He led her toward the dance pavilion where a band played soft music that curled around them as they moved together. Persy could feel the strength of his arms around her and the muscles in his shoulder under her hand. She closed her eyes and inhaled the scent of his woodsy cologne and the heavy fragrance of the surrounding gardenias. Putting her head on his shoulder, Persy rubbed her cheek against the cool fabric of his jacket.

After a few dances in which Persy felt she and Jordan were the only people in the world, Jordan said in a tight voice. "I guess it's time for you to meet my mother."

"Why do you sound like that? Is she so terrible, or don't you want us to meet?" Persy pulled away from him and looked into his eyes.

"No, she's my mother and I love her. The problem is that every time she meets my date, she starts planning a wedding." He held her hand and led her toward the mansion.

"Certainly you can set her mind at ease."

Jordan stopped in the shadow of a live oak and put his hands on Persy's shoulders. Looking deeply into her eyes, he said, "I'm not sure."

"What do you mean?" She was breathless, wondering what he'd say and how she'd react.

He laughed, breaking the serious moment, "I'm not sure what would set her mind at ease. Come on, let's go find her."

She wasn't difficult to locate.

"There she is, over there, in the silver dress. That's my mother, Cornelia Jordan Rutherford Prince."

Mrs. Prince stood out in the crowd. There was a regal bearing to the way she held herself, as straight as the dignified gentlemen who surrounded her, lantern light shining on stunningly coifed white hair and glimmering off a silver lamé dress.

"I'll bet no one ever called her Corney," Persy said. "How do you think she'd react if I did?"

"Please don't, I beg you. I know if I forbid you to do that, you'd do it to embarrass me in front of everyone here."

"There you are, darling." Cornelia Prince smiled at her son and held out a hand covered with diamonds. "Who is this charming young woman?" She moved away from the others so the three of them stood alone.

"Mother, this is my date, Persy Marsh. Persy, my mother, Cornelia Prince."

"You are quite lovely, my dear. Your name is . . . unusual. Is it short for Perseverance?"

"No, for Persistence."

"How interesting. Why would your parents name you that?"

"My parents believed in instilling values in us from the start. I have a sister, Diligence, and a brother named Fortitude, although he goes by Fort."

"What do they do, my dear?"

"My sister is a doctor and my brother is a concert pianist."

"What an exceptional family. What do you do?"

"I'm a dog walker at your hotel."

"Oh." Mrs. Prince took that well, Persy had to admit. There was barely a flicker of a change in her expression.

Mrs. Prince turned to Jordan and said, "Darling, please run along now. I want to talk to Miss Marsh, to get to know her better."

"Of course, mother, but don't keep her too long."

"We'll be fine. Go talk to all those people you need to talk with."

Giving Persy a smile, Jordan took a glass from a waiter as he was dismissed.

"Now, my dear, let's sit over here in this gazebo where we can be private." Mrs. Prince led her to a tiny summerhouse and motioned for her to sit on one of the seats lining the edge.

"Won't people disturb us?"

"No," Mrs. Prince said with calm confidence. "They won't. Not if they see I don't want to be disturbed." She looked at Persy and smiled, an expression that completely transformed her finely chiseled features. "He loves you, you know."

"Oh?" Persy blinked. "Why would you say that?"

"I've seen my son escort young women to dances and parties since he was twelve years old. You're the first woman he's truly been with. What I mean is that when he *escorted* other young women, he was there and the young woman was next to him but they weren't together. He's *with* you. You're *together*. He touches you. I can tell he truly cares about you."

"How do you feel about your son's affection for the hotel's dog walker?"

"Delighted, absolutely delighted. We Jordans are not good at showing emotion. I was afraid he'd never fall in love, that he'd be lonely all his life. I actually feared he had no heart to give. My dear, I can't tell you how happy you've made me."

"Really?" Persy's amazement showed in her voice. "But I'm no one. With all these rich, sophisticated, well-connected women here, how can you prefer me?"

"Ah, my dear, I don't prefer you. Jordan does and that's all I care about. Tell me about yourself. How old are you? I can tell you're an intelligent young woman. What is your educational background? I ask this so I can get to know you, please understand. You don't have to pass any test of mine."

"I'm twenty-five. I graduated from Stanford and have a law degree."

"Why don't you practice law?"

"After I passed the bar, I discovered that what I'd trained for—corporate law—wasn't what I wanted to do."

"You care for people more than business, don't you?"

"Yes. How did you know that?" Persy was amazed that this gentel woman, so like her own mother, could understand her so much better.

"Oh, it's obvious, my dear. I can tell a lawyer as soon as he or she enters the room—stiff, dull, egotistical. You're not one of them. And what about your family?"

"My father is a doctor. He practices in Arcadia. My mother is a doctor's wife."

"And what are your plans for the future? I mean, if you were to marry my son?"

"Oh. I really hadn't thought." Persy paused for a minute and let the marvelous joy of the thought roll over her. "I'm actually a community organizer in El

Valle. I'd probably stay there, in the neighborhood, and work on improving education and health care."

"Charming." Mrs. Prince took Persy's hand. "What a lovely thought. We Prince women pride ourselves on caring about others but we do it . . . oh, how should I say this? We do it from here." She waved her arm in the direction of the mansion. "Not that there's anything wrong with what you do but, perhaps, we'd all be happier if you did something with your law background."

Persy stiffened up. "*We'd* all be happier? Who do you mean?"

"Oh, dear. I have ruffled your feathers, haven't I? I know Jordan would never tell you this, my dear, and you do need to know. You could still be a lawyer and help people, couldn't you? If you were to become part of our family, we'd want you to—how should I say this?—fit into the society that surrounds you. Perhaps a public defender?"

Persy felt numb. "I really don't want to practice law, Mrs. Prince."

"Well, you think about it. Think about what would make Jordan happy and how you would fit in with us. With your background, I'm sure you'd be a wonderful addition to the Prince family."

"If I changed to someone else?"

"Oh, no, my dear. I'd never suggest that." Mrs. Prince stood. "Please come visit me again when we can have more time together. I feel sure you will. Now, I need to return to my guests and I'll allow you to return to Jordan. He is a dear boy."

"Yes, he is. I'm very fond of him, too."

Jordan was waiting for Persy outside the gazebo. "How did it go?" he asked.

"She's a lovely young woman, dear," his mother answered. "I feel sure I'll see her again." She smiled again at the two of them and rejoined the group she'd left.

"She's very nice. Not at all intimidating." Persy put her hand on Jordan's arm and allowed him to lead her around the lawn, still feeling worried and numb from Mrs. Prince's words. Certainly Jordan didn't feel that way, did he? He'd never said anything, never suggested she should change.

"Ah, yes, you're so easily intimidated."

"Well, no, but I do prefer it when people don't try it. Where are we going now?" She smiled up at him, trying to mask her feelings, deciding to enjoy the party and think about the rest later.

"Let's get something to eat."

When they got to the refreshment tent, Jordan said, "Have you ever tried these? They're my favorite." He pointed to a plate of marinated artichoke hearts stuffed with bleu cheese. "Or do you want to try the Mexican food tent?"

"I'm fine. This is more food than I can ever possibly eat. I'll need to take something home to Agatha."

They found a secluded table where they put down their plates. Jordan took Persy's hand and held it on the table between them.

"This makes it hard to eat." Persy attempted to take a bite of a chocolate truffle but couldn't because her plate kept moving away.

"I don't care. I want to hold your hand."

"In that case," Persy put her fork down, "let's hold hands."

"I don't think I've ever been as happy as I am tonight."

"What's so special about tonight?"

"I'm with the woman I . . . with the woman I . . . love."

"What?" Persy dropped his hand and jerked away. "What did you say?"

"I love you, Persy. There, I said it. I was afraid I'd never get the courage but it wasn't even that hard. I love you, Persy."

"Jordan, I don't know what to say." His mother was right about his loving her. Was she right about everything?

"You don't have to say anything. I'm not asking how you feel. I want you to know how I feel. Now, my love, will you dance with me? I want to show everyone this beautiful woman is with me."

My goodness. He loved her. A niggling thought intruded. Had he told her he loved her because she looked good? Because he could show her off like a trophy? "I'd love to, Jordan, but I . . ." she stopped. What could she say? Suddenly her stomach began to churn and a headache smashed into her left eye. "I'm really not feeling well."

Jordan looked down at her, his eyes filled with concern. "You are looking pale. What happened?"

"Food I'm not used to? Excitement? I don't know. It just hit me."

"Oh, Persy, I'm sorry. Let me take you home."

"You don't want to miss your party. You have people you need to talk to. Perhaps a cab?"

"Oh, sure, why don't I have a chauffeur take you home? That's the way we Prince men treat women—especially the women we love." He put his arm around Persy's shoulder and led her through the crowd. Stopping at one of the tents, he gestured to one of the servers. "Greene, please tell Mother I had to leave, would you? Miss Marsh isn't feeling well." They continued toward the front of the house. "Greene is one of the indoor staff. He'll make sure Mother knows."

"You should be back quickly. I don't think I'm going to be a lot of fun. When we get home, I'll go to bed. Agatha will look in on me."

They got in the car and Jordan pulled her close against him and put his arm around her. She didn't want to fuss or cause a scene so she stayed within the warmth of his arm and tried to relax away the headache that confused her thinking.

"I guess this means no more loving tonight?"

"I think you can say that. I've found watching one's date throwing up isn't conducive to romance."

Jordan looked down at her but she couldn't see his expression. His muscles tightened. "You're not going to throw up now, are you?"

"Don't worry. I'll warn you."

The rest of the drive passed in silence. Her stomach had stopped pitching when they reached La Paloma but her headache had settled in for a long stint. She knew this pain well. It was one of the worst parts about being Mary Persistence. Stress, always stress. Trying to live up to someone else's expectations, attempting to be who she wasn't, always brought them on. In high school, they'd been constant. At one time, she'd thought everyone lived in such agony, but her best friend Phyllis had looked at her wide-eyed when Persy asked her how she handled the headaches. Phyllis had helped her understand their pain wasn't normal and why she had them. Persy had figured out how to avoid them.

Until now.

Jordan helped her from the car and up the steps, ringing the door for Agatha because Persy couldn't find her key.

"What is it?" Agatha snarled until she saw the slumping Persy. "Oh, let me help you." She opened the door and motioned Jordan toward Persy's bedroom. "You can help her to her room, young man, but don't you stay there. It's not proper. You leave her there and I'll take care of her."

If she had felt better, Persy would have laughed at Agatha's tone. Instead, she sank onto the bed, kicking off her shoes and laying her head back on the pillow.

"I'll feel better if I can rest a little." She smiled weakly up at Jordan. "I'm sorry to ruin the evening."

"Take care of yourself." He held her hand so tenderly that Persy wanted to forget her concerns. Of course he loved her.

"I'll call in the morning." He leaned down and kissed her cheek as she closed her eyes, then tiptoed from the room.

"Do you need any help?" Agatha grumbled from the door.

"No, I'm feeling better. Can I call if I need you?"

"Of course. Never refused to help a person in distress. Don't much like to but never have refused."

Persy allowed herself to relax, forcing her tight muscles to loosen and saying the same words that she'd found effective as a teenager for ridding herself of the pain. When she was able to open her eyes without fearing that her head would topple off, she stood and stared at herself in the mirror. She'd forgotten she could look like this—glamorous and sophisticated, even if a little green—although appearances had been very important to her not so long ago. She turned from side to side and admired the formerly chic but now slightly disarrayed beauty she saw there.

"He said he loves you," she said to the image in the mirror, "but does he really love you or does he love the you that you were tonight?" Persy went toward her reflection and touched her hair. The sophisticated wave was beginning to bounce back into tiny curls. Had he thought he loved her because she was elegant and polished?

Persy glanced up at the glamorous stranger in the mirror. He'd never told her he loved her until tonight, when she looked like his type of woman: poised and refined.

Persy considered what Mrs. Prince had said. She believed Jordan loved her but she also wanted to turn Persy into Mary Persistence, exactly like her mother.

Stop it, Persy told herself. *He loves you. Even his mother said he does.*

Her thoughts wouldn't be quiet. *Who does he really love?* Persy the dog walker or Mary Persistence the well-bred beauty? The truth rushed upon her and almost crushed her. He only told her tonight he loved her; only tonight when she was gorgeous and looked like his kind of woman did he tell her. He must think he could mold her into the type of woman who would fit the Prince image. That's the woman he loved. Not

Persy of the goog-goog-googelly eyes. Not Persy who beat him in baseball. Not the Persy with the tinkling cocker spaniel. None of those Persies. He'd laughed at those Persies. He only loved Mary Persistence, the one in the fashionable dress with the normal hair.

Oh, darn! Ignoring the pain the jarring movements caused, Persy tore off the dress and threw it on the floor. She picked up her shoes and threw them forcefully into the closet, tearing off her stockings and tossing them in after the shoes.

She should never have left her own world. She knew all the pain in that other world, the one represented by Jordan and his family and her own family.

She took the earrings off and placed them carefully on the dresser, then slipped a nightgown over her head.

What a fool I've been, Persy thought. To think he'd ever love silly me. To fall in love with him when he was falling in love with someone else, the me he wanted me to be. The me his mother wants me to be.

Who ever would have thought that she, herself, would be Jordan's other woman?

"I could be that woman," Persy whispered. It wouldn't be hard. She could buy some nice clothes and have her hair styled. She could be the Persy that Jordan wanted. She could do that because she loved Jordan—yes, she really did—and wanted to be with him in whatever form he wanted her to be.

Of course, she'd also become Mary Persistence, the woman her mother wanted her to be. The Mary Persistence who suffered from migraines for years, unbearable pain because she couldn't bear the life she was stuck in.

No, not even for Jordan could she go back to that. She looked at her reflection again before she took out tissues and cream and wiped off all the makeup. After than, she opened the drawer and took out a pair of scissors. Without stopping to consider the consequences, she began cutting the waves until her hair was so short that tiny curls clustered all over her head, so uneven it would be weeks before she could ever look glamorous again—or even presentable, she realized.

That should remind her—and him—who she was.

The tears started to come but she stopped them. What was she going to do?

Her headache had subsided greatly when she discovered its cause but she knew it wouldn't go away until she severed the relationship.

She sat down at her tiny desk and started a letter:

Dear Jordan,
Thank you for the wonderful evening. I feel that you and I are too different for anything to work out between us. I've decided it is best not To see each other again.
Best wishes, always.
Persy Marsh

She read it to herself. It sounds a little stiff, she thought, but on the whole, it expressed what she wanted to say. She folded it carefully—for some reason, it was very important that all the corners match exactly—and slid it into an envelope. Licking it shut, she wrote "L. Jordan Prince" on the front. She looked out the window and could see the bright lights illuminating the passageway between the hotel and El Valle and knew she wouldn't sleep until she completed the task. Taking off the nightgown and throwing on a pair of shorts and a T-shirt, she slipped her feet into sandals and left the house to walk alone across the newly poured cement and up to the hotel.

"Paul, would you please make sure Mr. Prince gets this?" She handed the envelope to the night clerk.

"Sure, Pers, I'll put it in his mailbox. You know how compulsive he is about checking that."

With that, she returned home, pulled off her clothes, and drew on the nightgown again before crawling into bed. It was a long, sleepless night and she dozed only fitfully but at dawn the headache was almost gone.

Chapter Eleven

"**P**ersy, darn it! Come out and talk to me now."
The words and the sound of pounding echoed through
Persy's restless sleep.

She fought to free herself from the enormous weight
that was holding her down. With tremendous deter-
mination, she forced her eyes open, then shut them
against the bright sunlight that fell across her face.
"Go away!" she shouted as she turned over. But the
pounding didn't stop. Her mind cleared and she realized the heaviness on top of her was only a quilt. She
pushed it off and struggled to sit upright. During all
this, she was aware that someone continued to hammer
on the front door and shout angrily until at last there
was silence. "Thank goodness," Persy thought, but she
wasn't going to be allowed any more sleep.

"Persy," Agatha called from the bedroom door.
"Jordan's here to see you. He seems very angry."

Persy looked at the clock. Eight-thirty. She'd over-
slept and would be late to work. Why in the world

was she thinking such ridiculous things when there was a very angry man—who was, in fact, her boss—in the living room?

She stretched. She must have gotten to sleep after all but didn't feel a bit rested.

"Tell him I'll be there in a minute." She threw her feet over the side of the bed and stood. Groggily, she stumbled to the mirror where she blinked and shook her head in an attempt to wake up. There she was: silly hair, big eyes, as Jordan had said. But this time the silly hair was grotesque and the eyes were red and swollen. She assaulted her hair with a brush but it didn't help. Picking up her robe, she shrugged into it and wrapped it around her—no need to dress up for Jordan now—and went into the living room.

"Persy, what the hell is the meaning of this letter?" Jordan turned toward her. "And what have you done to your hair?"

"I cut it." Persy peered around but Agatha wasn't in sight. Had she disappeared due to cowardice or discretion?

"It looks horrible."

"I know." She frowned. He looked wonderful. His trousers were light blue, fresh and beautifully pressed. The tie matched his yellow shirt and dark jacket. It wasn't fair that he looked handsome and immaculate when she felt and looked so terrible. Of course, he hadn't been up crying all night. The injustice made her even grumpier.

"Why did you cut it?"

"Because I didn't want to look glamorous."

"You certainly succeeded." He waved an envelope. "Persy, what does this letter mean?"

"It means I don't think we should see each other anymore."

"Why? Because I told you I love you?"

"Partially."

"What does that mean? Did that make you feel trapped? I'm not trying to force a commitment from you. I love you and I wanted to tell you. I'm willing to give you room to see how you feel."

"No, that's not it."

"Well, what is it? I'm really getting tired of trying to guess what the problem is. Would you mind taking part in this conversation?" Jordan's voice got louder.

"It's not a conversation. You're yelling at me." Persy sank down in a chair. "Men! You're always trying to intimidate . . ."

"Let's not make this a battle of the sexes. This is between you and me, not men and women."

"Okay, but don't yell!"

"I'm upset! Why did you write this letter?" Jordan paced around the small room. "I thought we had a wonderful evening. Mother likes you. She called this morning to tell me again. Everyone there thinks you're beautiful and bright. What happened?"

"It's not that you told me you loved me. It's the timing and the reason you told me."

Jordan let out a long, deep breath. "Would you please explain that."

"You didn't love me like I was, plain and frumpy."

"You've never been plain and frumpy!"

Persy took a deep breath.

"Last night, you told me you loved me. You decided you loved me because I was glamorous and I fit into your world. I don't want to fit into your world. I left that world. I want to be me, not someone you want me to be. I can't go back to being Mary Persistence again. I refuse to live that way."

"What in the world do you mean?" He ran his hand through his perfectly coiffed hair.

"You know when I didn't want to talk to you about my past but Susan filled you in anyway?" When Jordan nodded, Persy continued. "As she probably told you, my family was well-to-do and I went to good schools and had high society friends and all that stuff. I didn't like it. No, I hated it. My family had horribly high expectations for me. I wasn't me when I lived like that. I refuse to be that way."

"Persy, I'm not asking you to live that way. I don't want you to change."

"But you didn't tell me you loved me until you saw that I could be glamorous and fit into your world."

Jordan sat down across from Persy and leaned toward her. "Persy, I didn't tell you I loved you before because those have to be the hardest words I ever tried to say. I'm thirty years old and I've never told a woman I loved her before, never! I've never been in love with a woman until you. The words didn't come easily. I wanted to tell you for weeks. The words got stuck in my throat every time I tried but they're true. I loved you when your face was purple. I love you now and at this moment you're the least glamorous woman I've ever seen."

"Thanks," she grumbled.

"Persy, that's not important. I was able to tell you I love you last night because I couldn't hold the words in any longer. Last night the words flowed. It was surprisingly easy."

"No, I can't believe that! I know you want to change me. You want to make me into a hostess and a society woman." Persy stood and moved as far away from Jordan as she could.

"What do I have to say to convince you? Yes, I admit, as the eventual director of the Prince chain, I'd like a wife that could help me with business but that's not a requirement. However, let me remind you, we weren't even talking about marriage. All I did was tell you I love you."

"That's why this is a good time to stop, before it hurts even more."

"I don't think it could hurt any more."

Persy looked up quickly. She hadn't even thought that she could hurt Jordan. "I'm sorry I hurt you, but I can't enter your world again, not for you or anyone."

"Persy, when you're in love, you have to leave your world. You have to enter the world of the person you love, at least partially. If I were to leave my world behind and live only in your world, I wouldn't be myself any more. I can't give up who I am for you anymore than I'd expect you to do that for me. That's part of a relationship: accepting the other person and accepting that person's world. You have to take a chance. You have to trust."

"I can't, Jordan. I can't. And your mother said . . ."

"I can imagine what my mother said. She probably expected you to become a perfect member of the Prince family. But I'm not my mother and I can handle her. I would never expect you to change to make her happy."

She stood looking at him, feeling wretched.

"What can I say, Persy, to make you understand?" he asked.

"Nothing, there's nothing you can say. I can't be what you want in a woman."

"Haven't you heard a word I've said? You're already the woman I want." His voice got louder and he enunciated the words carefully, pausing between each.

"You're yelling again. Please don't yell."

"Persy, stop behaving like such an idiot."

"I'm not behaving like an idiot. You're an imbecile."

"Now you're shouting, too." Jordan closed his eyes and seemed to be trying to calm himself. When he spoke again, his voice was quiet. "I didn't care what you wore. If you'd put on that flowing thing that you wore on our first date or even your Phantom of the Opera outfit, I wouldn't have minded. I don't care how you look because I only want to be with you. I always think you're beautiful, even now. You're the one who decided to wear that black dress and fix your hair that way"

"I know. I made a terrible mistake."

"Wait. First you said it was my fault now you say it's yours. You can't change your point of view in the middle of an argument."

"Yes, I can."

"Women! You are so . . ."

"You said don't make this a male–female fight. You can't change the rules in the middle of an argument!"

"Yes, I can."

They looked at each other. Both were red-faced. She was quivering, he was tense.

"I don't think there's anything more we need to say to each other. Please leave." Persy pointed toward the door.

"I know where the door is." He turned toward it. Before he left, he said, "Don't forget we've got that interview Friday. I'll have a limo pick you up."

"No, I couldn't possibly . . ."

"You're going to have to, Persy. You're an employee of the hotel and I expect you to behave that way. You don't have to like me to appear on television and promote the recycling program."

"Yes, sir. I'll be there. I'd appreciate the limo."

"Goodbye."

This time he left and Persy threw herself on the sofa face down.

"Well, that was some display." Agatha came into the living room. "What in the world have you done to your hair"?

"I cut it."

"Why?"

"I didn't want to look glamorous any more."

"You've taken care of that."

"I know, but, Agatha, I'm so miserable."

"I don't doubt that. You've behaved like a spoiled brat, but I don't suppose you want to hear that now or to let me try to even up your hair. When you're ready, let me know. Go take a shower. You'll feel better. I'll fix your breakfast."

Torn between her belief that a shower wouldn't help and the dread of sitting in the kitchen with a judgmental Agatha, Persy decided to try to control the damage. "Just toast. I don't feel like more."

"Nonsense. Go shower."

"Would you call Martha and tell her I'll be in late?"

The water felt wonderful, reinvigorating her, relaxing her shoulders and clearing her head, although it was immediately filled with more tumultuous thoughts. She stood under the warm spray and twisted her shoulders, wishing her pain and confusion could be worked out as easily as her muscle tension.

When she got out of the shower and was rubbing her hair dry, she glanced in the mirror. He used to love the way her hair became little curls, she thought, but now it seemed as confused as she was. Here and there were little curls but in other places the tufts stood up straight. In a few patches there didn't seem to be much hair. With a sigh, she dried the rest of her body and pulled on jeans and a T-shirt.

Breakfast mirrored Agatha's disapproval. With the nearly burned bacon and the runny eggs, it suited Persy's mood. She nibbled at the crusts of the very dark toast.

"I'm going to take the bus up to visit Burt. I'm leaving in a few minutes. Do you want to talk before I go?"

"You heard everything."

"Okay, be that way. I'll leave you to stew."

Persy nodded and continued to eat.

"I'm ready to leave now." Agatha picked up her purse.

"Fine. When will you be back?"

"Before dark. Don't worry about me."

"I will," Persy gave her a trembling smile. "I know I'm being a brat but I can't seem to help it. I will worry about you if you're not back on time." She stood and gave the older woman a hug. "I'll miss you. Have a nice time."

Agatha sniffed.

Persy dreaded work and didn't want to pass Jordan in the hall or see him in his office when had to talk to Martha. Fortunately, she didn't have to worry. The board meeting started with a luncheon at noon. Persy sneaked into her cubicle and called Martha to check in.

"I can help you all day, Persy, if you need me to," Martha said over the intercom. "I worked very hard last week to get ready for the board meeting. Mr. Prince will be in business sessions all day today and tomorrow."

"He won't be coming by the office?"

"No, he's too busy when the board's here."

"Okay, I'll be right there. I've got some letters and memos that need to go out." At least, Persy thought as she walked down the hall, work did help keep her mind off her problems.

Persy dreaded the sound of her phone ringing. Sitting in her tiny cubicle, she felt alone and safe. The phone brought messages from the outside. "Hello?"

"Hi, Pers, this is Hogan. I need your help. We're really short-handed today. Please help serve lunch to the board at noon."

"Oh, no! Not that! Hogan, I can't."

"Pers, I know you're not a waitress anymore. You're a big important executive . . ."

"That's not why, Hogan."

"But I wouldn't ask if it wasn't important. This is my job, Persy, my neck. Everyone called in sick. They all went to a party last night and got food poisoning. Maria's the only person that could make it in. I've called everyone I can think of, Pers. If you can't help, I'm dead. Think of my wife and kids—ten little children."

"Okay, I'll be there, but last I heard you had one son. Do you have a uniform I can wear?"

"Sure. Thanks, Pers."

This is going to be terrible, she thought, but it wasn't too bad. She was filling tea glasses when Jordan and the board came in. She saw him stiffen slightly, then walk to a chair, ignoring her. Mrs. Prince wasn't there, thank goodness, and none of the other directors recognized her. Of course, they'd never imagine that this waitress with the peculiar hair was the Cinderella of the previous evening. Her dream had definitely turned into a rotten pumpkin.

As Hogan arranged the plates coming off the dumbwaiter, she and Maria served salads.

"Lovely young woman you were with last night," one of the gentlemen sitting next to Jordan began as Persy put the salad down in front of him.

"Thank you, sir. The numbers on the . . ."

"You're much too serious, Prince. Exactly like your father. Don't talk business during lunch. Let's talk about that beautiful young woman. Looks like she comes from our kind of family."

"Yes, she is lovely. Tell me about your wife. I'm sorry she didn't come with you."

"Why do you keep changing the topic, Prince?"

Persy moved on down the table but she could still hear the conversation in the small room. "Well, look at this. That waitress looks like that young woman, except there's something wrong with her hair."

In an even voice, Jordan said, "That waitress is my

date from last night, sir. As you know, she works at the hotel. I guess she must be filling in for another employee today."

"Is that right, Miss?" the board member asked her.

Hotel policy forbade talking to guests, but this was a board member. How could she ignore him? She nodded, "Yes, sir."

"That's impressive. She can do anything, can't she? Fine young woman. Makes a good wife." In a loud whisper, he asked, "What did she do to her hair?"

"I don't know, sir. Didn't I hear that you caught an enormous fish out in the Gulf last week?"

Well, she thought with a sigh, everything is going fine. It proves Jordan and I can work together professionally and not even care about what happened last night or last week.

Dessert was strawberry shortcake. Hogan was putting the strawberries on the cake while Persy covered them with whipped cream from a dairy can.

"How's everything going in here?" Jordan asked from the door.

Startled to hear his voice so close, Persy turned, her finger still on the top of the can. Whipped cream sprayed across Jordan's face and down the front of his shirt before she could gain control of herself.

"Oh, no! Jordan, I'm so sorry. You surprised me." She wanted to reach out and wipe the mess from his eyes but knew she couldn't. "I'm sorry. I'm so stupid." Her voice quivered. "I don't do this to anyone else. Only to you. I'm so sorry."

"That's comforting." He tried to clean his face with his fingers. "Persy, are you crying?"

"No, of course not. I never cry. You know how

tough I am." She turned around and tried to wipe the tears with her apron.

"Persy, stop. I can't stand to see you . . ." He took a deep breath. "Persy, calm down and finish serving the guests. I'll go downstairs and change." He took a towel to wipe his eyes before he left the serving pantry.

"You do get yourself in some fine fixes, don't you, Pers."

"Hogan, if you only knew."

The house was lonely, Persy realized when she opened the door at five-fifteen. This was what it would be like when Agatha left. She'd be alone. "I need to find someone else to live here with me," Persy said aloud. The sound of her voice in the empty rooms surprised her. She wandered back to Agatha's room and looked in but didn't enter, respecting Agatha's privacy. Agatha would take her odds and ends but had promised to leave the furniture: a nice double bed, a double dresser, a mirror, and a bedside table. Agatha's cat statues covered the dresser and her books took up the shelf in the nightstand. The pictures on the wall were of nieces and nephews. When Agatha left, the walls would be bare, the shelves, vacant. The house would be empty and Persy would be alone again.

It was, of course, her decision, one she'd made years ago and stood behind. She had to be herself. She couldn't give up her principles, even if she made herself miserable.

Could she?

* * *

The next night, Agatha was watching television in her room when Susan knocked on the front door.

"I've got something I need to talk to you about. Can I come in?"

"Sure." Persy opened the door and motioned Susan into the living room.

"I have a cousin coming to school here next fall and she's looking for a place to stay. With the four boys, I don't have enough room or any privacy for an eighteen-year-old female. Do you know anyone with extra space?" Susan settled herself on the sofa and looked up at Persy. Her eyes opened wide when she focused on Persy's hair, but she said nothing.

"Sure. How about here?"

"Here? You mean, in your house?"

"Yes, of course, in my house. Agatha's moving and I'm planning to take the larger bedroom. Your cousin can have my old room."

"What about you and Jordan?"

"What does he have to do with this?"

"I thought you'd be married by September."

"We're not dating anymore."

"What?" Susan blinked.

"We broke up last night. Actually, this morning, early." Tears started rolling down Persy's face, although she refused to give in to sobbing. "Actually, I'm very happy about this. I think it's for the best."

"Yes, I can tell. I've never seen you more radiant."

"We're too different. There's no way we can ever work this out."

"I have to admit, I didn't like him much before you started dating. I wondered why in the world you'd go out with such a stuffed shirt, but now I think he's a doll. He obviously adores you. You're so much alike."

"No, we're not." Persy protested loudly.

"What's the problem? Don't tell me he's going out with someone else. I wouldn't believe it."

"No."

"Then what?"

"He wants me to be glamorous."

"Persy, you are such an idiot. If I didn't love you so much, I'd whop you upside the head! But you're an adult and I'll leave you to live your life. I'm not going to interfere, but it'd be nice if you'd think like an adult instead of a little kid."

"Thanks."

"I've been trying to be polite . . ."

"Telling me you want to whop me upside the head is polite?"

"But I saw you last night. You *were* glamorous. You looked like a princess with her prince," Susan said.

"Yeah." Agatha suddenly stuck her head in the doorway and said. "Only this princess stomped on the glass slipper. Shattered it into a thousand pieces."

"Persy, how . . ." Susan turned toward her friend as Agatha slammed the bedroom door behind her.

"I don't want to talk about it. I can't put the pieces back together again. Lord, that's Humpty-Dumpty. Why are we talking about a bunch of children's stories?"

"Because you're acting like a child."

"Thank you for your support and interest." Persy sat very straight and held her chin up. "Can't you think of another topic you'd like to discuss? Another one of my shortcomings?"

"Well, I didn't want to ask this but it's killing me. What on earth did you do to your hair?"

Jordan tossed the keys in his hand. He stood in front of the fourplex but didn't go in. He closed his eyes and swallowed as the vision of those babies—his and Persy's babies—disappeared into the warm breeze blowing across the Gulf. It was just as well. It was a good thing he found out how wacky she was before they had all those babies, those beautiful babies with the crazy blond curls and big blue eyes. Darn, they could break a man's heart and they weren't even born yet. Would never be born.

He almost smiled, remembering the stiff idiot he'd been only a few months earlier. He'd thought he had no heart to give. Now he felt like the cowardly lion. He knew he had a heart because it was breaking.

"Trying to decide what to wear to the interview?" Agatha stood in the doorway to Persy's bedroom Friday morning.

Persy turned toward her. "I think I'll wear that suit my mother sent. Do you think that would look okay?" At Agatha's nod, Persy continued, "Would you work on my hair and see if you can get it at least presentable?"

She'd worn a baseball cap the previous day so people wouldn't ask, "What have you done to your hair?" Instead, they'd asked, "Why are you wearing a baseball cap?" It was obvious she couldn't wear one on television.

"Sit down." Agatha picked up the scissors and began snipping in an attempt to even the ends. "What made you decide to act like a responsible adult for once?"

"Well, it's my job. Besides, I believe in the recycling program and that means I have to look and do my best on television to sell it. I need to be professional."

"Well, you're showing a little sense." Agatha ran a comb through Persy's hair. It was still short but everything seemed to be curling in the same direction. "You don't deserve it but you still look adorable and innocent." She snorted. "Very deceptive."

Agatha came around to look at Persy from the front. "Don't understand why you're so angry with that man. He never asked you to change for him. You changed yourself."

"I know. That's why I'm frightened. I'm afraid that, once I start to change because I want to please him, I won't be able to stop and I'll be my old self again."

"Not Jordan's problem. It's yours."

"Agatha, I'm scared to death. I don't know what to do to be able to be with Jordan and stay myself."

"Yes, you do know, but you're so darn stubborn you won't do anything about it. Don't come crying to me about it." She shuffled out of the room.

"For the interview, please sit on the loveseat there. I'll be asking each of you questions about this new project of the Gulf Prince Hotel." Marian Fairborne, host of the morning show "Good Day, Gulf City," escorted Persy and Jordan to the loveseat and motioned for them to sit.

Persy took the right side and plastered herself against the arm of the loveseat. Jordan sat on the left, comfortable and relaxed but careful to stay on his side of the pillows.

"I'm going to ask you a few questions, alternating from one to the other. Have you been on television before, Miss Marsh?"

"No."

"Jordan, I know you have. We had that great interview about the charity ball last spring."

"It was a lot of fun."

"We'll be taping and would like to get it in one take, if possible, but if you do make a mistake, we can always retake. We'll be showing this Tuesday morning. Now," Marian studied them for a moment. "You're sitting a little far away from each other. Miss Marsh, could you scoot a tad to the center of the loveseat?" Persy moved perhaps a quarter of an inch. "Oh, no, more than that. Could you move almost to the middle, Miss Marsh?"

Persy looked up at Jordan. At his nearness, she'd almost stopped breathing. It wasn't fear, she assured herself, but couldn't define the emotion that filled her.

"I'm sorry, Miss Marsh. Is this making you uncomfortable?"

"Oh, no, Ms. Fairborne. Is this all right?"

"Well, you're still a trifle far apart. Jordan, move in a little on your side, closer to the middle."

Jordan slid an inch across the cushion until Persy's glare stopped him.

"Well, that's a little better." Marian contemplated the positions. "You see," she pointed, "we have the emblem of the station on the wall behind you and I've never seen so much of it before. Most of the guests cover the bottom part of it, but now it's there, sort of sticking out between you. It's a better shot for our cameras and looks great on television to have you against the colors of the emblem." When neither moved, she asked, "Is there a reason you don't want to sit close to each other?"

When Persy's face whitened, Marian hastened to add, "Oh, I'm sorry, I didn't mean to be personal."

"Yes, there's a reason, Marian. I told Miss Marsh that I love her and she's very uncomfortable with it."

Persy gasped and turned toward Jordan with flashing eyes.

"You've finally fallen in love, Jordan? That's hard to believe . . ."

"Have I made you angry, Miss Marsh?" Jordan asked in a harsh tone, interrupting Marian—if he'd even noticed she'd been talking.

"I'm trying to be professional, as we discussed. I don't believe we need to talk about the intimate details of our private lives with anyone." Her voice was low, the words coming through clenched teeth.

"Yes, that's fine, Miss Marsh," Marian mumbled. "You sit however you feel most comfortable." She moved away from the set and the growing tension. "We'll start the taping in a few minutes."

"Would you feel more comfortable if I put my arm around you and pulled you over close to me? That should break the ice." Jordan placed his arm across the back of the loveseat.

"No, I'm fine." Persy moved away from his arm as if it were covered with maggots.

"Your hair looks better this morning. Short, but it suits you."

"Thank you. Agatha evened it up for me."

"How are her marriage plans?"

"Everything is fine. She's getting married tomorrow."

"Yes, I remembered the date." He kept his eyes on her face, inscrutable but searching.

"We're all going in Susan's car." Persy looked away from him, pretending to find something of great interest in the camera lens. Why couldn't he leave her alone? Didn't he know how hard it was to be next to him? Couldn't he feel the signals of yearning that she was sending out, completely against her will.

It wasn't fair that he could be so handsome and desirable and so calm that anyone watching would think they were buddies, old pals, chums. Anyone who was insensitive enough to not feel the almost pulsating waves of attraction that surrounded them.

"Give her my best. She's a grand old girl," Jordan said with a friendly grin. As if there were nothing between them.

They said nothing more. Persy had frozen in her position away from Jordan's arm and she sensed he felt a perverse pleasure in her discomfort.

"Tape starts in thirty seconds, Miss Fairborne," one of the technical crew said.

"Ready, Miss Marsh? Jordan?" Marian moved to sit in the chair opposite the loveseat.

"Ready in five, four, three, two . . ." The technician pointed at Marian. When he did, Jordan removed his arm and Persy leaned back in the loveseat.

"Good morning, Gulf Coasters. This is Marian Fairborne with 'Good Day, Gulf City,' sponsored by Walker Shoes. Remember, 'If you're going to walk, choose a Walker.'

"My guests this morning are Jordan Prince, manager of the Gulf Prince Hotel, and Persy Marsh, director of Ecological Projects for the hotel. Good morning to both of you."

"Good morning," both said with wide smiles and cheerful voices as the camera shifted toward them.

"Would you please tell me, Mr. Prince, the reason the hotel decided to begin the program."

"Miss Marsh is very good with her facts—in some areas. She was able to convince me by stating statistics that recycling can make a difference. After all, having the most beautiful, best-staffed hotels in the world doesn't do us much good if the landfills are so full there's no place for our trash."

"Miss Marsh, how did you become so interested in the environment?"

"About three years ago, I began to realize that we're all responsible for . . ."

When Persy completed her statement, Marian looked into the camera. "We'll be right back with more about this exciting new program after a few words."

"I think that's going very well." Marian noticed neither was listening to her again.

"What do you mean I'm 'good with facts, in some areas?' " Persy demanded.

"I meant exactly that. You know about ecology but you don't know anything about relationships. You can't tell the difference between truth and lies when it comes to how I feel about you."

"Those aren't facts. Those are emotional areas, not at all logical."

"Back in five, four, three, two," the technician counted down and pointed. Persy mouth snapped into a grin as the camera panned the set.

"Marian Fairborne, back with Persy Marsh and Jordan Prince. Tell me, Miss Marsh, what are some of the projects you have in mind?"

"We're beginning with inexpensive recycling efforts." Persy explained for a minute.

"Now, about the costs, Mr. Prince. How do you pay for these projects?"

"Much recycling pays for itself and more through money saved. When we do make money, such as through selling aluminum cans, that money will go toward the Green Alliance of the Gulf. When we contemplate new projects, the expense will need to be considered. For example, if we add solar panels to heat water, how much can it heat? Will it be able to meet the needs of a three-hundred-room hotel?"

"Will it be cost-effective?" Persy added. "That's always an important question with Mr. Prince." She leaned toward Jordan at the same time he shifted position. His arm brushed Persy's shoulder and she leaped away as if he'd burned her. "Don't . . ." she began, then took a deep breath and regained control. "Don't forget that there are other considerations than cost."

"Unlike some people, who are unable to consider anything objectively, who don't have to pay for . . ." Jordan began in a calm voice that grew louder as he talked.

"It's been extremely interesting speaking with the

two of you," Marian interrupted as the tension built again. "I hope you'll accept our invitation to come back in six months to tell us about the progress of this project."

"We'd love to," Jordan said woodenly.

"Delighted." Persy nodded stiffly.

"And out," the technician said.

"Well, thank you. I think it's fine. It certainly was an interesting, lively show. Let me check with the booth . . . yes, they say we're finished. Thank you for being here." Marian held out her hand and shook Jordan's and Persy's. "Goodbye."

"Goodbye, Marian, and thank you," Jordan smiled. "We'll need to get together again."

"Goodbye," Persy said politely and turned to leave the studio but before she could take three steps, Jordan's voice stopped her.

"Wait a minute. I have something for you." She turned and Jordan stood behind her, holding out a set of keys.

"What's that?" Persy made the mistake of looking up into his icy eyes before she rapidly lowered her gaze to the silver objects swaying before her.

"These are the keys to your dream, the fourplex."

"What? Why? When?" She glanced at him again but his eyes hadn't softened and his chin looked like granite. Obviously the sight of her didn't turn him into a quivering mass the way seeing him had done to Persy.

"I bought it for you a couple of weeks ago. No, actually, I bought it for us, but I don't have a use for it now."

"You bought it for us?" she repeated.

"Don't ask me why. Here." He tossed the keys to her. "I hope you enjoy it."

"Why?" she asked anyway.

"Because I loved you. Because I wanted to spend the rest of my life with you. I *was* talking about marriage. I changed while you and I were together, and I like the person I was with you. Thought maybe you wouldn't mind changing a little too, occasionally going to corporate parties with me, maybe entertaining from time to time. After that, we'd come home to our apartment and the kids. I don't have any use for it now. You might as well have it." He turned on his heels and walked away.

"Jordan, I can't . . ." But he was gone as her voice trailed away.

She couldn't, simply could not take such an expensive gift from him. She looked up to follow him but, as he was leaving, Marian had stopped him. The newswoman had her hand on his shoulder. Jordan's head was lowered to listen to her.

Now, *she's* glamorous, perfect for him, Persy said to herself. Tall, thin, wearing a plain but obviously expensive and very fashionable beige dress. That's what he wants me to look like.

Even as she thought it, Persy knew that wasn't true. Once they'd started to date seriously, he'd never cared what she wore or how she looked. This whole thing wasn't his problem. It was hers. She was jealous of those gorgeous women of his past and feared she'd destroy herself competing with them, trying to look like them, making herself be like them when he'd fallen in love with *her*.

She wanted to go after him, apologize, tell him it

was all her fault and that she'd . . . well, she'd do something but she didn't know what. She realized that, as confused as she was, she had nothing to offer now: no solutions, no suggestions.

Persy looked at the keys in her hand. He loved her—well, he said he *had* loved her and he hadn't wanted to change her. How stupid could she be?

She might not have a answer to everything but she could at least thank him and apologize. Then they could work this out together. Surely they could work things out—if she'd stop being such an idiot.

Great hope flowed over her. She looked up, tears mingling with a smile, starting to move toward Jordan just in time to see him leave the building with Marian.

Chapter Twelve

Persy looked at the pile of boxes in the room. All of Agatha's possessions were packed in those boxes and tomorrow she'd be gone. "Do you have everything? Are you sure you're not leaving anything behind that you'll need or that's yours?"

"Yes, dear." The drawn and occasionally dour look was gone from Agatha's face, replaced by a smile of joy and anticipation. "Burt and I won't need all that kitchen stuff. We'll be eating all our meals in the dining room. Now, these boxes." Agatha motioned toward three by the door. "I want Frank to put those in the back of the car with my luggage. Those are the things I want to take with me. The other boxes I'm going to store in the closet and I'll let you know when to bring them up. I won't need them until we move into the bigger apartment." She smiled and shook her head. "I'm so excited. I feel like a new bride."

"You *are* a new bride. I'm so happy for you."

"I am happy." Agatha looked into Persy's eyes. "I wish you were happy."

Persy made a brushing motion with her hand. "Don't worry about me. I'm fine."

"I don't like the thought of you being alone."

"I won't be alone. Barbarella and I'll be happy here together."

"That's not what I mean."

"I know."

"But you don't want to talk about it. I don't know why you're worried about Jordan. He's the most honest, decent man I've ever met, after Burt. You know he'd never ask you to give up your independence, but you don't want to talk about him."

"No, I don't. I made a terrible mess of things because I'm so stupid."

"I wouldn't say stupid." Agatha sat down and pulled Persy next to her on the bed. "Bullheaded and stubborn."

"You're right. I've made such a mess and I don't know what to do about it now."

"You're not an idiot. You know what to do."

"No, because I'm bullheaded and stubborn, exactly like you said."

"Bah. You can change."

"See, that's the conundrum. I can change or I won't change or I shouldn't change or no one should ask me to change or I stay myself. Which should it be?"

"Sometimes you're too darned smart for your own good."

"Don't I know it." Persy shook her head before she stood. "Now, let me press your dress and hang it up. The bride must look beautiful."

*   *   *

"Dear friends, we are here to celebrate the joining of this man and this woman in the blessed and consecrated institution of marriage," Chaplain Madeline Walters began. The ceremony took place in the chapel of the center. The minister stood in front of a communion table covered with blue and white flowers surrounding flickering candles.

Facing the minister was Agatha, glowing in her new blue dress and holding a beautiful bouquet of gardenias. Next to her stood a tall and smiling Burt.

The minister looked at Agatha and said, "Agatha Smith Norton, you have come to this holy place to become the wife of Burt Alan Robertson. Will you make your pledge to him?"

"I promise to be your wife," Agatha said as she turned to Burt. "Through whatever time we have together, to love and care for you . . ."

Persy watched Agatha and listened to the words of promise and love. As much as she tried to ignore the feelings swirling inside her, Persy wished she were standing there with Jordan, stating what she knew but was afraid to admit aloud.

Why was she such a stubborn idiot?

Tears began to roll down her face and she dabbed at them with the tissues Susan passed to her.

When the minister turned to Persy for Burt's ring, the tears kept flowing, continuing even after the chaplain pronounced Burt and Agatha husband and wife. Persy followed them down the aisle and into the parlor for the reception, one hand on the arm of Burt's son while she wiped at her tears with the other.

"I really am happy for you," Persy told Agatha.

"I know." The older woman patted Persy's hand before she turned to greet Frank and his brothers, Burt's family, and the few other guests.

As the couple accepted the best wishes of their friends, Persy watched them. Agatha couldn't stop smiling, an expression Persy hadn't seen before Burt entered her life. Agatha's joy had blunted her grumpy remarks and changed her caustic personality. Amazing what love could do. The observation started Persy's tears again.

"I always cry at weddings," Persy explained when Susan handed her another handful of tissues.

"Yes, we've noticed how emotional you are," Susan observed. "Cry at the drop of a hat."

"Or a bridal bouquet."

"Are you going to throw it?" Susan asked Agatha.

"Don't know why I should. Persy's never going to get married, the way she's going, and you've already got a perfectly fine husband."

Well, marriage and happiness hadn't completely taken the sharp edge from Agatha's tongue.

"Oh, all right. Here it comes." Agatha tossed the flowers straight at Persy, who couldn't help but catch them.

Persy sniffed the gardenias and was immediately transported to the Prince mansion, dancing with Jordan's arms around her. "I must be allergic to the gardenias." She handed the flowers back to Agatha. "Please keep them, to remember today."

A few minutes later, Persy picked up a glass of punch. "A toast to the bride and groom. To Agatha and Burt: long life and a love to last eternally."

Burt touched Agatha's cup. "Long life, eternal

love," he repeated, looking at her with devotion shining in her eyes.

All in all, even though she was delighted for Agatha, it was one of the most wretched weddings Persy had ever faced.

"Well, I guess it's just you and me, kitty." Persy watched Barbarella hop onto the chair in which Jordan usually sat. The cat put her head down on the fabric and rubbed, attempting, Persy guessed, to find his scent.

"You miss him, too, don't you?" she asked, picking the cat up and trying to settle her in her lap. Persy scratched the cat's ears but she jumped away, meowing pitifully.

Sitting on the floor in front of Persy, Barbarella looked up at her, straight in the eye, and said, "Meow!"

"I know. I want him back, too."

Shaking her head, Barbarella said, "Meow!" very loudly.

"I'm not understanding your message, am I, kitty?"

Looking at Persy with disgust, Barbarella stood and jumped back on the chair.

"We both miss him."

With an insistent "Meow," Barbarella jumped from the chair and went to look out the front window. She put both paws on the window pane and stretched.

"The difference is, I can go get him but you can't."

Turning, Barbarella looked at Persy and gave a "Meow" that was obviously a nag.

"You want me to . . . ?"

"Meow." She sat down in front of Persy and began

to lick her paws and purr, as if content she'd gotten her point across.

"Well, of course. What could be simpler? That's exactly what I want, too." Persy began laughing. "Why in the world have I been so hardheaded and stubborn? I love Jordan. Even if he's fed up and disgusted with me and tells me to go away and leave him alone, I can't be more miserable than I already am."

"Meow?"

"Change?" Persy interpreted. "I guess I'll have to have faith in him and in myself."

Persy stood and ran out of the house. It was dark— almost eight o'clock. They'd returned home from the wedding only an hour earlier.

Persy dashed down the street, across the well-lighted walkway and up to the hotel. At the front desk, she stopped. "Have you seen Mr. Prince?"

"No, sorry, Pers. I've only been on a few minutes. Want me to call his suite?"

"Yes, please."

After a few minutes, the desk clerk said, "He's not answering, Pers."

"Thanks, Bob. I'll check his office."

"I can call."

"No, thanks." She was off as he spoke. "I'll see if he's there."

But he wasn't. The light was on and the door was open but there was no one inside. Persy entered slowly, calling his name, but no one answered. Papers were spread across his desk and the computer was on but he wasn't there. How strange, she thought, sitting down on the sofa and picking up a magazine to read.

Within five minutes, she fell asleep, relaxed after a long day and an exhausting week.

Jordan looked out the window of his office. He couldn't see La Paloma from here. He turned back to the desk, covered with work that he hadn't been able to concentrate on.

She didn't want him, didn't trust him. Why should he spend time thinking about her? It wasn't even eight o'clock. He had hours of work left to do. He needed to get the report in by Tuesday, but he couldn't focus on the numbers and words before him. Maybe a walk would clear his mind. Jordan slipped on his shoes and left the office, taking the back stairs to the parking lot.

He stood where he could see her house. It hadn't changed, of course. The lights were on but he couldn't see her. Of course, he was pretty far away. Perhaps he should go over and see her, to make sure she was all right. He bet she really missed Agatha and could use the company.

He walked down to the house and knocked on the door but no one answered. He saw Barbarella inside but no one else.

"Darn," he muttered before turning around and ambling back through the passageway to the parking lot. As he walked, he kicked a box that blew in front of him. It felt good. Relieved a little tension. A little further across the parking lot, he saw a paper bag and gave it a good kick.

Pain erupted and filled him. He fell on the asphalt and braced himself against waves of agony and nausea. When his head finally cleared, he touched the bag and attempted to pull it toward him. It wouldn't move.

Pushing himself with his good foot, he crawled the short distance to the strange sack.

A cement block. Some joker, a deviant mind, had put a cement block in the sack, hoping for someone to do what Jordan had done.

He looked around but there was no one in sight. *Great, what am I supposed to do?* he wondered. He tried to stand but his foot wouldn't cooperate. Falling back on the asphalt, he closed his eyes as pain rolled over him.

"Mr. Prince?"

He turned to see one of the maintenance men standing over him. "I'm going to need some help, Nelson. Get a car and drive me to the hospital."

"Shouldn't I call EMS or an ambulance?"

"Nelson, this isn't an emergency. Get a car. By the way, I'm glad to see you. Thanks."

Nelson drove to the emergency room, parked, and got a wheelchair from the hospital to push Jordan inside.

"I think I broke my foot," he told the admitting room clerk.

"Take the chair over there," he said. "Fill out your paperwork. We'll get to you as soon as possible. We've had a bad traffic accident tonight so we're running behind."

At eleven-fifteen, he was still waiting. His doctor wasn't home and the on-call resident suggested he wait for the orthopedic resident. He'd sent Nelson home at nine and was sorry he did. The man was good company.

Jordan picked up a magazine. It was in Spanish. He picked up another: *Mother and Child.* He picked up a

Readers' Digest from 1985 and began reading the stories he'd skipped the previous two times he'd perused it. "There should be an 'I am Jordan's Foot' article," he muttered.

"Mr. Prince?" a nurse called him through the window. "Please come back."

The doctor took a quick look and asked for X-rays, which were almost unendurable.

"Well, the good news is it isn't broken, Mr. Prince. Lots of damage in there but no broken bones. We'll wrap it up. Keep off it and come back Monday to see a specialist. I'll give you some pain medication. Actually," he said after a pause, "as much pain as you must be in, and with all this damage, we should keep you in the hospital. You'll probably need surgery. Nurse," he called into the hallway, "have Mr. Prince taken up to a room."

"No!" Jordan sat up and shouted. "I don't want to spend the night in the hospital. That's why our medical costs are so high: too many people who don't need to be here spend time in the hospital." My gosh, he thought with surprise, I'm getting to sound exactly like Persy.

"If that's what you want. Make sure you get back here Monday to see Dr. Estrada." With great care and gentleness, the doctor wrapped the foot. "Here's some pain medication to hold you. It's going to make you sleepy, so don't drive. How are you going to get home?"

"I'll need a taxi."

"Is there someone to take care of you? You can't move around on that foot."

He thought for a moment. "Yes, there is," Jordan

said with conviction. Heck, Persy took in every stray in the neighborhood. why shouldn't she take him too?

It was 2:30 A.M. when he arrived at Persy's house. For a large tip, the driver helped him to the door. The light was still on and Barbarella still sat inside, meowing.

"Is she working, kitty?" By this time, the medication was making him feel a little odd and he was almost surprised that Barbarella didn't answer him. "I'll sit here on the swing until she gets home. I'll wait up for her right here, kitty."

He hopped over to the swing and tried to sit down, almost falling on the porch when it moved away from him. With a one-footed leap he was on the swing. He scooted around until he was partially lying down with his foot on the arm of the swing. He fell asleep immediately.

The pain in Persy's back woke her at three. Where was she? Slowly, she realized she'd fallen asleep on the sofa in Jordan's office. She stood, stretched, and yawned. Obviously, he wasn't there.

Was he out with Adrienne or Marian? Maybe he was already dating and here she was waiting for him in his office. How pathetic. She'd never kiss him or laugh with him again. She might as well go home.

She turned out the lights and closed the door on her way to the back steps. She was halfway across the parking lot when she saw that she'd left a light on in the house. As she got closer, she saw something or someone on the porch, lying across the swing.

Who was it? What was it? Was someone hiding

there to attack her? Whoever it was hadn't done a very good job of hiding. Why would someone be waiting for her there?

Maybe it wasn't a person. Maybe it was a large package. She slowed down and walked past her house, trying to make out what was on the porch swing.

It was a person, but who? Why? There was a terrible noise coming from the person. She sneaked along the property line to the edge of the house, picked up a branch, and worked her way to the porch.

"Who is it?" She held the branch up threateningly.

There was no answer except the rasping sound, which frightened her with its spooky loudness.

"Who are you and what are you doing here?" she shouted.

There was still no answer. Should she get Frank? No, she had the branch to protect herself, and she'd scream if there was a need. Silently, she went up the steps to the porch and tiptoed around behind the swing. Under the overhang of the roof, it was too dark to see who was there, so she pulled the back of the swing and dumped the person onto the floor.

"OOOOOOOOW!" The scream was frightening. "What was that? Who did that?"

"Jordan?" He wasn't out with some glamorous society woman. He was on her porch at three at night. Why?

"Persy? Where've you been? Don't step on my OOOW!"

"What's the matter?" She dropped on the floor next to him.

"Hurt my foot. May need to have surgery next week."

"Oh, Jordan." She lifted his head in her arms. "But why are you here?"

"Figured you could take care of me," he mumbled.

"Why didn't you stay in the hospital?"

"Medical costs, all that stuff, you know. Please take care of me, Persy."

"Of course I will. Let me help you inside." When he started to try to stand, Persy put her hand on his chest. "No, you stay here until I open the door. Then I'll help you."

"You're a little bit of a girl. You can't lift me."

"We'll do this together. You know how strong I am. Stay." She stood, unlocked the door, and threw her purse inside. "Let me get my hands under your arms, like this. Okay, now lift. Don't put your weight on your foot. Okay? Up? Do you feel steady? Now, put your arm around my neck and hop."

She took him into the house and gently let him settle on the couch. "I'm going to go back and get the bed ready. You stay here."

"Where else would I go and how would I get there?" He giggled. "Sit down next to me. Need to talk. I love you. I want to marry you. Please." Barbarella jumped into his lap and stretched to lick his face before curling up on his leg.

"Yes, love." She took his hand. "I'm sorry for everything I did, for how stupid and stubborn I was. I love you. I was wrong."

He yawned. "Medicine makes me sleepy. Waiting and waiting for you. Where were you?"

"I was in your office. I was waiting for you, to tell you I was wrong and that I love you."

"Silly hair, silly eyes." His head began to nod before he jerked awake again. "Will you take care of me?"

"Of course I'll take care of you. Now, you stay here and I'll get your bed ready."

"Okay." When Persy stood, he put his hand out and took her wrist. "I love you."

"I love you, too. I'm going to put you to bed."

A look of pure bliss came over Jordan's face. "You're going to put me to bed?" He fell asleep before she could answer.

Persy went back to Agatha's room, took linen and a spread from the closet, made the bed, and folded the sheet back.

"Okay." Persy shook Jordan awake with great effort. "Can you stand up for me?" She moved the cat, took his hand, and pulled him up. "Keep off that foot. Okay, put your arm around my neck. Let's go."

"Persy, take care of me. Without you, I'll go back . . ." He swayed against her. "What was I saying? Oh, I'll go back to being that shuffed stirt . . . no, that shtuffed . . . I don't want to go back to that other guy, Persy."

"Yes, darling, I won't let that happen." She helped him through the door and onto the bed. "Let me take off your shoes. I mean your shoe. Do you know where your other shoe is?"

"Do you know where your other shoe is?" he repeated.

"Well, you can afford another pair." She took off his socks, then unbuttoned the knit shirt and pulled it over his head, marveling again at his broad chest— but this was *not* the time. When she looked at the trousers, she realized she'd have to slit the leg to get them off.

"Just a minute. I have to take your trousers off."

"Persy's going to take my trousers off," he sang with as much joy as his bewildered condition allowed. "Just what I want. Thank you, Persy. Thank you, thank you."

She cut the seam all the way to the waistband before carefully sliding the trousers down his legs and past his bandaged foot.

"Take care of me, Persy. I like me when I'm with you. If I'm not with you, I'll be that other guy again. Don't want to be that other guy again. Want to be with you."

Persy arranged his legs carefully on the bed. "Are you comfortable?"

But he was asleep. As she watched him, Barbarella jumped on the bed, purring loudly and turning around and around to make a nest on the blanket.

He looked so marvelous, so dear. With a sigh, she flicked the light off and went to the front of the house. After locking the door, she went back into her bedroom and began to undress. She hung up her jeans, threw the dirty clothes in the hamper, and slipped a nightgown on.

As she turned down the sheets on her bed, she thought, *how ridiculous*. She dropped the covers and left the room, tiptoeing into the other bedroom although she knew Jordan was asleep and nothing would wake him up for a long time.

For a moment she studied him again in the dark, then pulled Agatha's chair next to Jordan and settled down on it, propping her legs on the bed. Barbarella looked up at her and meowed. "It's okay, kitty. We're going to have to share him."

Persy smiled at Jordan as she fell asleep, wonderful thoughts for their future together tumbling through her mind.

The small house on La Paloma, cooled by a salty breeze from the Gulf and lit by the orange and pink rays of sunrise was filled with dreams, dreams about Persy and her prince.